ICED OUT

A DARK ENEMIES-TO-LOVERS HOCKEY ROMANCE

BLACKWOOD BLADES
BOOK ONE

ISLA VAUGHN

ARROWSCOPE PRESS, LLC

Iced Out

(p) ISBN-13: 978-1-951919-75-7

(e) ISBN-13: 978-1-951919-74-0

Publisher: Arrowscope Press, LLC; www.arrowscopepress.com

Editing— Taylor Anhalt, Editor

Cover Illustration—Audrey Anhalt https://audreyanhalt.com

Cover Design—T.E. Black Designs; www.teblackdesigns.com

Interior Formatting & Design— Arrowscope Press, LLC; www.arrowscope-press.com

PROLOGUE

MILA

One year ago...

The text from Mom came while I was still at the rink watching the boys' varsity hockey team practice. Just one line: *Can't make dinner. Don't wait.* It didn't sound like her.

By the time I pulled into our driveway, the sky was streaked in bruised purple, red, and gold. Her car wasn't there. She didn't answer my calls.

The unease in my chest coiled tighter, sharp enough to hurt.

That sixth sense I'd learned to trust in every town we'd ever lived—it screamed that something was wrong. I opened her location on my phone. A single blinking dot lit up the map—King Enterprises.

It was after-hours, and she shouldn't have been there. Fifteen minutes later, I pulled into their nearly empty lot. The glass building rose up in front of me, all mirrored windows and steel edges reflecting the last of the sun. King Enterprises looked domineering even in the best weather, but under the heavy shadows, it felt colder. More ominous. Only a few lights glowed inside. I should've left. Driven home. Pretended I hadn't seen where she was.

But I didn't.

Her location showed she was behind the building. I cut the engine and stepped out of my car. The walk around the building felt longer than it should have. The air back there was cooler, heavier, carrying the faint scent of motor oil and something copper, metallic. The industrial lights along the wall flickered in uneven pulses, slicing the concrete into shifting bands of shadow.

I spotted Mom before she saw me—long dark hair spilling down her back, shoulders rigid, that familiar tilt of her head. My eyes tracked past her… and caught on the prone shape of a man lying on the ground.

The building blocked part of him, but I could see enough— the wrong angle of his limbs, the red pooling wider by the second. My breath snagged. A scream clawed up my throat.

Mom spun at the sound, and her eyes locked on mine, intense and unwavering. She closed the space between us in two quick strides and clamped her hand tight over my mouth.

"Not a sound," she hissed, her voice a razor-edged whisper. She darted a glance over her shoulder then locked urgent eyes with me. "We have to move."

My pulse pounded so loud it drowned the distant hum of traffic. My knees trembled, barely holding me up.

Because I knew who it was—Darren. The guy Mom had been dating. The VP at King Enterprises. The man whose lifeless eyes—eyes I'd seen crinkle in laughter just weeks ago— stared past us into nothing.

"Mila." My name carried a sharp panic that cut through the fog in my head. I tore my gaze from Darren's face and locked on hers.

"We have to go. Now. Get in your car and move. I'll meet you at the house. Hurry."

I ran. My legs didn't feel like mine, my breath scraping in and out as I slid behind the wheel. The drive home was a blur of headlights and static, my hands gripping the wheel until my knuckles leeched of color.

When I skidded into the driveway, she was right behind me. Her car door shut, and the front door was open before I'd even killed the engine.

"Pack," she snapped. "Everything you need. Bags, boxes, I don't care. Just move."

"What? No. We need to call the cops—"

"No cops." Her voice cracked like a whip.

"But we didn't do anything—"

Her gray-green eyes locked on mine. "It will come back to us. You have to trust me. The people who did this—" She broke off, fingers curling against her side. "They'll put it on us. Do you understand? They *will* make sure we take the fall."

It didn't make sense. But Mom had always looked out for me. And every line of her face, every tight coil of her body, screamed *run*.

I grabbed bags, stuffing them without thought. Jeans. Hoodies. My sketchbook. The framed photo of me and Luke from last summer at the lake.

Luke.

An ache tore through my chest. Just a few hours ago—after practice, when the ice still clung to the air and the locker room was empty—I'd slipped my white-gold chain with the tiny star pendant into the side pocket of his hockey bag. A good luck charm for his away game tomorrow. I'd wanted him to find it later, know I was rooting for him, that our future was written in the stars. It was supposed to be something I would get back after the game, when I could listen to every detail straight from him. I already missed the weight of it against my skin.

He wasn't just my boyfriend—he was every breath, every steady thing I'd ever believed in. If I could just hear his voice, maybe I could breathe again.

My fingers hovered over his name on my phone. Mom's hand closed around my wrist before I could type.

"Under no circumstances," she said, voice low but fierce, "can you text about what you saw. To no one. Not even Luke. Especially Luke. He can't know why you're leaving. Or even that you are."

Tears stung my eyes, blurring her face into something soft and unfamiliar. "Mom—"

"Promise me, Mila."

My chest ached. The words scraped out, raw and splintered. The future we'd planned and dreamed of shattered around me. But Mom had always looked out for me. And in this, I had to believe she still was. "I promise."

I thought I was protecting him. Turns out, I was setting the fuse.

CHAPTER ONE

MILA

Present Day

I clenched my fists as Mom pulled into the driveway of our new rental—a squat, forgotten house slouched behind overgrown hedges and broken dreams. The porch sagged under the weight of peeling paint and rust-bitten railings. Weeds clawed through the concrete like the place was trying to swallow itself whole. It looked temporary. Like us.

Blackwood. The name hit with the force of a punch to the ribs. The town I swore I'd never set foot in again. And yet, here I was.

Mom threw the car into park as if she hadn't just driven us headfirst into a land mine. Her exhale was light, as though she hadn't ripped the scab off a wound I'd spent a year trying to forget. Another town. Another house. Another mask to wear. But this wasn't just another pit stop on our escape route. This was the origin story of every broken piece inside me.

Luke King. The name pressed against my skull, relentlessly. I forced it down. The next time I see him, he wouldn't be the guy I remembered. The one who kissed me as if I was air and he couldn't breathe without me. I didn't need to see him again to know that boy was gone, no doubt replaced by someone colder. Crueler. The kind of dangerous that didn't need weapons because of who he was and who he was connected to. Someone I'd helped create by leaving the way I had. As if I'd taken his trust and thrown it back in his face.

I'd left him without a goodbye. Just one message on a phone I wasn't supposed to have. *I'm leaving. I'm sorry.*

He'd called. Texted. Begged. Then raged. Until I went dark. Changed my number. Disappeared. But now, we were back. Walking willingly into the heart of the storm.

"Mila, help me with these boxes." Mom broke my mental spiral as she popped open the door, stretching as though this was a yoga retreat instead of a return to hell.

I grabbed the nearest box, shoulders stiff. Arguing with her wouldn't change anything. It never did. Our life was built on burned bridges and fabricated names. She called them reinventions. I called them what they were—lies dressed in fresh coats of paint.

This move wasn't about reinvention. It was a resurrection.

Supposedly, someone had offered her a job too good to pass up—financial consulting, high-dollar, low-transparency. She swore it was clean. That it had nothing to do with the past, with how she'd worked for King Enterprises back then, or what'd happened. No one had come after us; she said we were good. Said her new job was with King's competition. But in Blackwood, every job came with strings. And I'd learned the hard way that those strings were often nooses.

The stairs creaked as if they knew we didn't belong. I walked down the hall and entered my room that was more storage unit than sanctuary—yellowed blinds, warped wood floor, air thick with dust and a ghost of something sour. Probably mildew. Possibly regret.

I dropped my box by the bed and turned to the window—and froze.

Beyond the rusting fence, past cookie-cutter houses trying too hard to be charming, loomed Blackwood Academy. All glass and stone. Cold and perfect. A castle built to keep people like me out. And just past it, the glint of metal and glass caught the light—Blackwood's prized rink. Luke's domain.

I knew before we got here that he still ruled it. His name was legend. His scowl immortalized in championship photos and whispered hallway threats. His family's empire was intact, at least on paper. But the cracks had started a year ago. And now, here I was, a sledgehammer with a fake smile.

Stay invisible. Graduate high school. Get out.

The plan was simple. And impossible.

The scent of cardboard and old pine cleaner filled the hallway as I ventured out of my room. Mom was already unpacking as if this place was a home instead of a strategic hideout. I found her in the kitchen, stacking chipped plates.

Her voice floated in, light and familiar. "We just got here. Thanks for checking in."

I stepped in as she leaned against the counter, casual and composed. Her eyes flicked to mine—intense and unreadable, too calm for a woman who just reentered enemy territory. She hung up the call.

I scowled, irritated on principle by everything. "Who was that?"

"Just someone from the company. Checking in."

"Bullshit."

Her smile didn't reach her eyes. "Don't start."

I took a step forward, tone razor-edged. "Tell me the truth.

Did we come back just to run again? Is there a new boyfriend turned potential payload waiting in the wings?" I was tired of it all—the new relationships that inevitably went wrong and resulted in us packing up and hightailing it out of whatever town we'd squatted in.

Her face shuttered. "I told you. This is the last time. You'll finish school here. Blackwood opens doors—"

"It also opens graves," I said, low and flat.

She flinched, barely. But I saw it.

Her hand landed on my shoulder with the weight of punctuation. "Have a little faith."

I stared until she dropped it. Faith had no place here. Not after last time. Because last time, someone died. And Mom acted as though the Kings hadn't pulled the trigger.

I'd gotten there after it happened. She'd seen more than I had. Then her hand had clamped over my mouth, my body shielded by hers as she got me the hell out of there. We couldn't be seen. I knew it just as much as she had. She had more information about that night than I did, even though I'd seen enough.

Her hands had trembled when she packed. She flinched at shadows. And she wouldn't tell me who pulled the trigger, just hinted at who was there. It was enough to buy my silence. This town has a ruling order, and crossing them was detrimental.

I followed her deeper into the kitchen, watching her stack another plate into a cabinet that looked ready to collapse. For the hundredth time, I pushed for the real reason we'd returned. "Why here? Why now?"

Her back stayed to me. "It was time."

"That's not an answer."

"It's the one I have," she said, her tone clipped enough to make the air feel colder.

Mom was my ride-or-die. The one who could read me without a word and make me laugh even when everything was falling apart.

At least, that was how it used to be.

But ever since she'd gotten word about this job, something had been off. The easy camaraderie, the I've-always-got-your-back steadiness vanished. She shut me out, held me at arm's length.

My chest felt like it'd been hollowed out by her words, and I curled my hands into fists. "We ran for a reason, Mom. Did that just… go away?"

She turned just enough for me to catch the flash of warning in her gaze. "You'll be fine if you keep your head down. Focus on school. Let me handle the rest."

"That's not what I asked."

"It's all I'm saying."

I frowned. "Blackwood Academy is expensive. How are we affording it? I thought we blew through our savings."

"Mila, please." Her shoulders tensed. "I've got it handled."

My stomach twisted. Memories, dark and blurred at the edges, crept in like smoke. Blood on the ground and sightless eyes. I'd spent the past year burying it all beneath a new school. But trauma didn't vanish. It waited.

And here, in Blackwood, it waited with teeth.

I didn't wait around for another excuse. I retreated to my room, dropped onto the mattress, then pulled out my phone, opening the *Blackwood Blades* page.

My heart skipped a beat, and my stomach flipped. There he was. Luke. Sin wrapped in varsity pride. The kind of guy whose name girls tattooed on their ribs as if it were scripture. The one they warned you about but followed anyway. He hadn't changed. If anything, the edge was sharper. The jaw more brutal. The confidence? Still weaponized.

Theo. Jax. Chase. Still beside him. As though nothing had ever happened. Like I was never here. Theo's dirty-blond hair curled just past his ears now, windswept and effortlessly perfect —he always looked like he walked off a magazine cover, and he knew it. Jax stood solid at Luke's right, dark-brown hair cropped tight on the sides, a little unruly on top. His green eyes scanned the crowd as if he was already looking for a fight to finish. And Chase—Avery's twin, blond and blue-eyed, broader than I remembered—leaned against a tree as though it owed him something.

I tapped over to Avery's page. Chase's sister. My once-friend. We'd been inseparable—until I ghosted her along with everyone else. She'd tried calling. Messaging. She even found my new number somehow. But I cut her out like everyone else, ditched the phone and used a burner from there on out.

Still, part of me hoped she'd remember. That some flicker of that friendship remained. But she'd moved on. Bonfires. Group shots. Homecoming prep. Her smile was bright and whole and surrounded by people who didn't ask questions.

They had lives. I had silence. I absently touched my neck, missing the comforting weight of the delicate white-gold chain anchored by a single star. My fingers curled around nothing—just skin and the ache of memory.

Luke gave the necklace to me after our night under the stars. It was a symbol of that shooting star we'd seen. Of distant fate. Of hope we didn't say out loud.

I'd left it for him, thinking he would find it and know what it meant. But we left that night. No goodbyes. No warning. I never got it back. And there was no way he would have kept it. Right?

I tossed the phone onto the bed and sat back, the cheap springs creaking beneath me. My eyes drifted toward the window again, to the shadow of the academy and the glowing lights of the arena just beyond it.

That ice had seen too much. Our first kiss. His first fight over me. The last time we spoke face-to-face. I remembered the sting of his words. The heat of his grip. The way the air fractured between us as though something sacred was breaking.

And now I was back.

The plan was to be invisible. But Luke never let things lie. Not when he felt wronged. Not when the past left scars that still stung.

This time, I wasn't scared of what he would do to me. I was scared of what we might do to each other.

CHAPTER TWO

LUKE

The first day of senior year, I hit the main corridor flanked by Theo, Jax, and Chase. The hallway split like the damn Red Sea. Heads turned. Conversations halted. Even the ones who hated me kept their eyes low.

One more year. Then I was out.

Not that college would be better. But it would be something else. Something *mine*—not preordained by my father or tied to the legacy of the King name. If I made it that far.

We moved as a unit, shoulders brushing, our presence too loud for anyone to ignore. Theo threw a lazy grin at a passing cheerleader who blushed and tripped over her own feet. Chase zeroed in on some sophomore he'd probably already hooked up with over summer break. Jax stayed quiet—watching, always watching, his mood unreadable behind the sharp lines of his face.

He was the only one who might understand the noise in my head.

My mouth was dry. I barely registered the girls whispering near their lockers, or the way teachers stood a little straighter when we passed. It didn't matter. None of them mattered.

Hockey did. Or it used to. It had been everything—was every-thing—until she left and took the hope I'd had for something different with her.

Plans I'd made to rewrite the story—mine, hers, ours—disin-tegrated the second she vanished. That was a year ago, and I still hadn't figured out how to bury the ache she'd left behind. I'd tried. God, I'd tried. But some wounds preferred to rot from the inside.

We turned down the final hallway, and the sea of students shifted again. A ripple of tension followed us like smoke. I didn't stop it. Didn't acknowledge it. Power, when wielded right, didn't need noise.

I was captain of the undefeated Blackwood Blades. Heir to a kingdom built on silence and blood. No one questioned me. No one dared. Until her.

A flash of long, wavy dark hair at the far end of the corridor stopped me mid-step. My pulse kicked hard. A familiar tilt of the head. The curve of a cheek I knew as well as my own reflec-tion. *No.*

My chest hollowed. It wasn't the first time I thought I saw her. Hell, I saw her everywhere. In dreams. In crowds. On the ice. My brain liked to torture me with ghosts.

But this wasn't a trick. The crowd split again, and she turned. *Mila.*

The world snapped to silence. And there she was.

My breath hitched like I'd been shoved. Air refused to find the bottom of my lungs. For a second, I couldn't tell if the sound cut out or if the sparking weight inside my chest had simply muted everything else. The lights blurred at the edges. Faces dissolved into a wallpaper of motion. It felt like I'd been pulled under and there was no surface.

She stood maybe twenty feet away, her shoulders straight and chin high. Same dark waves tumbling down her back. Same full mouth that used to whisper truths against my skin.

Her gray-green eyes scanned the crowd, not landing on me. Not yet.

I should have moved. Heat crawled up my spine, my hands going numb at the fingertips. A prickled cold started at the base of my skull and spread down, sharp and electric. My vision tunneled until I could see Mila and nothing else. I could see the line of her jaw, and the little scar that freckled the curve of her collarbone.

Panic tightened a fist around my throat. It didn't make sense —I'd trained for games that mattered, for finals that decided seasons. But this was different—older and meaner and wrong. Old plans and promises I'd buried—the ones I'd swore I'd never speak—rose like tidal water and tried to wash me away.

There are rules, I told myself. King rules. Captain rules. There was no fracturing in public. I couldn't look weak, or give away anything that someone could use against me.

So I did what I'd always done—I moved. Slower than anyone would notice but with mechanical purpose.

Hiding didn't stop the tremor though. It just made it smaller —contained in a chamber behind my ribs. I pressed my thumb into my palm until it hurt while counting. If Mila saw, she could peel the bandage back and show the wound like it was some trophy. The thought made something hot and ugly climb up my throat.

I slid into the bathroom and quickly closed myself off in one of the stalls. Locking the latch, I leaned my head back against cold metal until the edges of the world stopped spinning. I breathed in—three quick, shallow breaths—then out, forcing a slow even push of air that wasn't there. My ribs felt like they were closing in. I thought about calling Drew or smashing the first mirror in my path. I even thought about the stupid star charm I'd kept in my bag and how heavy it had been the night she left me with it.

I couldn't crumble. I would not hand her that power again.

I'd had to learn how to make the pain useful—turn it into ice, into focus. But none of that stopped me from remembering that rooftop and her telling me to fight for the future I wanted.

By the third set of inhales, I could feel the edge of the panic dull. The tremor stayed, a low engine vibrating under my skin, but the world was righted enough to function. I unlocked the stall and caught a glimpse of myself in the mirror. A vein in my temple visibly throbbed. I scrubbed water over my face, slammed the faucet off, and smiled at myself in the mirror—almost feral.

When I headed back out into the hallway, I carried anger like a shield. Panic had been private and useless; anger could be wielded. I let the heat harden into something that would look like motive to anyone watching. Jax threw me a look—questioning, not accusing. I shrugged like nothing was wrong.

The panic had been a hole I could step around. Anger was a weapon I could drag across everything that stood between me and an answer.

My hands curled into fists at my sides. I forced them to relax. Forced my face blank.

She wasn't supposed to be here. Her silence meant she was never coming back. But there she was—walking my halls as if she belonged and hadn't shattered me into pieces and ghosted like I was just another mark.

I couldn't think past the roaring inside my head. She was back. And she looked exactly the same. Like she'd never left. As if the last year of wreckage meant nothing to her.

And suddenly—brutally—I was back on that rooftop with her.

It had been past midnight, the town stretched out in lights and shadows below us. She'd sat between my legs, back against my chest, wrapped in one of my sweatshirts three sizes too big. Her fingers played with mine, slow and distracted, as if she already knew what I was going to say.

"I don't want to take over King Enterprises."

She didn't react. Not immediately. Just squeezed my hand, grounding me.

"I know," she whispered.

I let out a breath. One I'd been holding since I was old enough to understand what my last name meant. "He's already decided. Has the board groomed to welcome me the second I turn twenty-two. Summer internships. Dinner meetings. The way he talks, it's as if it's already done. I don't get a choice, despite my brother being the firstborn."

"And hockey?" she asked, voice small.

"That's mine," I growled. "The only thing that's mine."

She twisted in my arms until she was facing me, her expression open and raw. "So fight for it."

"He'll cut me off." But that wasn't the real problem. My dad and his circle didn't just control—they owned, ruled through blackmail, bribes, and a full arsenal of quiet threats dressed in tailored suits. If they wanted a business, they took it. People either fled or got hurt.

"Let him." She shrugged as if it was that easy. "You'll find another way."

"And if I fail?"

She smiled then. Soft and fierce and terrifying. "Then you'll fail knowing it was your choice. Not his."

I stared at her, this girl who came from nothing and had more courage in her pinky for her future than I'd ever been allowed to show. Her reaction settled something in me—she didn't care about my legacy, about money. It was me that mattered to her. Her eyes were lit up with belief—*in me*. As though I could take down empires with a stick and a dream.

I leaned in and kissed her—slow, reverent. Like maybe she was the only real thing in my life.

"Stay with me," I'd whispered into her skin. "Don't ever leave."

Her answer had been yes. Over and over, in kisses and sighs and the way she fit against me as if she'd been built to.

Now, that same girl was walking down my hallway like none of it had happened. I stepped forward before I even realized I was moving. "You've got to be kidding me," I muttered.

She didn't hear it. Didn't see me yet. But she would.

She turned the corner, vanishing into the crowd again before I could get closer. It didn't matter. This wasn't over. Not even close.

If she thought she could walk back into Blackwood as if the past didn't exist, like she hadn't carved me open and left me bleeding, she was dead wrong.

I was done playing nice. First stop: the front office. It took ten minutes and a look at the receptionist that dared her to challenge me. Mila's schedule.

We didn't share a single class. Not a problem. That would change this week. I'd already submitted a request for course adjustments. Being a King had perks. She wouldn't be able to take a piss without me knowing about it.

By the time I got to calculus, my blood was still running hot.

The classroom buzzed with lazy conversation. A few people scrolled on their phones. Some hovered by desks, catching up on bullshit that didn't matter.

Jax, Chase, and Theo had already claimed our usual spot in the back. They spread out, owning the place—because we did. We didn't ask for space. We took it.

I dropped my bag beside Jax and stretched, pretending like I gave a damn about math.

"Everything good?" Jax asked, voice low. His broad shoulders took up more space than the other two.

He didn't look at me, but his tone held weight. He felt the shift.

"Fine," I said. It was a lie. But he didn't push. He rarely did.

Chase shifted in his seat, stiffening beside me. His attention snapped to the doorway. That predatory stillness meant one thing—he saw something he didn't like.

I followed his line of sight. Avery. My jaw ticked.

His sister walked in laughing, shoulder bumping against Mark Delaney's like it belonged there. His hand hovered at her lower back.

Wrong move.

Jax caught the shift too. His mouth curved into something dangerous. "Problem with your sister talking to that guy?"

Chase tensed. "Mark's not good enough for her."

To us, no one was good enough for Avery, but her brother took that to extremes.

"Didn't ask if he was good enough," Jax said, voice calm but edged. "Asked if it was a problem."

Chase muttered under his breath then stood like he was about to start something. Jax leaned back in his seat, amused.

I didn't stop Chase. He could handle it. I had my own shit to deal with. Because Mila being back? That wasn't a coincidence. No way had she returned without a reason.

Last time she saw me, my world was crumbling. My dad caught her mom in something—money, theft, who the hell knew. All I got were fragments and fury. My father said they ran because she was guilty. That her mom screwed us over and Mila helped.

And when she left without a word? I believed him. I let myself believe she was just like the rest—using me until it didn't serve her anymore.

But now? Now she was back. And she didn't get to pretend nothing had happened. She didn't get to keep my secrets, disappear, then walk these halls like she hadn't gutted me. This time, I'd make damn sure she stayed. And she would answer for what she did.

Seeing Mila knocked the air out of me. And it only got

worse when I caught her bare neck—no chain, no star pendant. Just skin where her promise used to sit.

She wore it every damn day. Swore she never took it off. That it reminded her we were real, even when everything else felt fake.

And now? Gone.

I hadn't thought about that night in months—no. That was bullshit. I thought about it every day. Just got better at burying it under everything else. Practice, school, meaningless hookups.

But seeing her now, seeing her without it? That chain wasn't just missing. It was a declaration.

The necklace she'd returned was still in my hand when I got back to my room the night she left. Silver, thin, delicate—but heavy in ways that had nothing to do with weight. The charm caught the overhead light like it didn't know it had been gutted of meaning.

My mind tripped back to when she left it for me with no explanation. No goodbye. Just slipped it into my hockey bag before an away game and walked away. Didn't even look back.

When I realized she was gone, that leaving the necklace with me was her goodbye, I stood there, a dumbass, fingers curling around the last piece of her I had, wondering if I should throw it. Smash it. Melt it down and forget she ever wore it.

My brother Drew found me. Door half open. Bottle of whiskey dangling from my hand and half gone. Me standing in the middle of the room with my knuckles white around a broken promise.

His eyes flicked from the chain to the bottle. "This isn't the way."

"Don't start," I muttered.

But he didn't flinch. Didn't get preachy or pissed. Just stepped inside and shut the door behind him as though he'd been there before. As if he knew exactly what it meant to watch someone you love vanish without a reason.

"I've been exactly where you are," he said, voice low, steady. "World turned upside down. Gutted from the inside out. And I promise you—it doesn't end with just one night."

I wanted to tell him to fuck off. That I didn't need a babysitter. But there was no pity in his face—just truth. And coming from my brother, truth held weight. He'd crashed and burned before—alcohol, drugs, rock bottom. Dad hadn't done much besides get pissed at the spiral Drew had fallen into. A disappointment. A risk. The pressure had shifted to me. If Claire—Drew's assistant back then, now his fiancée—and I hadn't dragged him out of whatever devastation had tipped him over the edge… I wasn't sure he'd have made it back. He still hadn't told me what it was, but Claire was his tether to sobriety now.

He grabbed the bottle, tipped it into the trash until the last drop was gone, then plucked the necklace from my hand and set it on the desk like it deserved to survive this night. Even if I didn't.

"Hold on to that. Trust me—it's lighter than what's waiting for you if you don't get your head straight."

And damn if he wasn't right.

That was the night I stopped trying to drink my way through the burn. At most, one or two beers at parties. Water after wins. Not because I was clean. But because Drew showed me where that road ended—and I wasn't ready to lose more than I already had.

And maybe that was why I only let family close now. Because trusting anyone else? She taught me exactly how that ended.

CHAPTER THREE

MILA

I slowed just short of Blackwood Academy's doors, pressing my palm against the brick as if steadying myself for what waited inside. For a moment, the thought of turning back felt almost reasonable. No Blackwood and no Luke, no eyes dissecting every step I took.

The urge passed, and I straightened. I let my expression settle into something calm, the version of myself I wore so they didn't see the real me—the side that longed for things to go back to how they were between Luke and me before everything went to hell. My hand drifted to my throat before I caught myself. The bare skin there felt more exposed than the crowd I hadn't even faced yet.

Brave didn't mean reckless. It meant walking through those doors even with fear and dread crawling through me. I smoothed my shirt and stepped forward even if every cell in me knew Luke King didn't hand out second chances.

The moment I entered Blackwood Academy's halls, I felt it—that electric snap in the air, the prick of a thousand eyes carving into my spine. Whispers slithered down the hallways, curling around corners. Some curious. Most venomous.

I used to rule this world at Luke's side. Now I was its fallen queen, ripe for punishment and ridicule.

With my head high, I took measured steps, my spine locked tight even as my stomach twisted itself into knots. The weight of judgment pressed heavy, unspoken accusations stitched into every sidelong glance.

I made it through the first four periods without running into Luke, or his crew, or Avery—or worse, Elise Dunn, heiress to Dunn Industries, and her cackling clique. Small mercies. Blackwood royalty had scattered themselves across different schedules and electives, which meant I could breathe. A little.

I took note of the new hierarchy since I'd been here last. Elise had climbed the ranks in my absence. I'd seen it unfold over social media—each carefully curated post, every tagged party photo, her proximity to the guys, as though it were a throne she was born to inherit. Elise didn't just want the crown. She wanted to make sure no one remembered who wore it before her.

I didn't expect peace. I wasn't stupid. I just hoped to buy time.

That illusion shattered the second I stepped into the cafeteria. The energy shifted. Forks paused mid-air. Conversations stalled mid-laugh. It was as if the entire room exhaled at once—then held its breath.

There they were. The elite. Lined along the back wall, gods surveying their court. Luke's crew sprawled along the table, a painting come to life: Theo leaned back, grin too predatory, Jax stone-faced and calculating, Chase halfway through a joke no one dared interrupt. And Elise. Poised just close enough to their table to stake her claim, as if she belonged—like she owned it.

She spotted me and smiled, a blade unsheathed. Then leaned into one of her minions, her straight, black hair curtaining her round face, highlighting her doe eyes, and whispered something behind a manicured hand. A second later, the entire table erupted in laughter, jagged and rehearsed.

I didn't have to hear the words to know they were about me. Screw her. I grabbed a tray and moved like I didn't notice. Found the farthest table from the chaos and sat with my back to the wall, where I could see everything.

Then his eyes found mine. Luke. The second our gazes collided, something inside me clenched and frayed. His stare was heat and fury and history rolled into one brutal punch to the chest. Attraction and longing for what we once were rolled through me. And for a breath, it was as if nothing had changed. Like we were still us.

His expression hardened. He looked past me, and I was once again invisible. And still, I felt it—the moment he stood. The scrape of his chair, the shift in energy as his team clocked him moving and mirrored him, shadows at his back. He cut across the cafeteria with one singular focus. Me.

I didn't move. Wouldn't. My gaze tracked him—every inch of his frame sharper than I remembered. He'd grown broader, thicker through the shoulders. The cut of his jaw was more defined now, honed by a year of pressure and pain. And I knew him well enough to spot the twitch—right there, beneath the corner of his jaw. A tell. He was spiraling. And I was the reason.

He stopped in front of me, crowding my space, the rest of his crew settling, a pack behind him. The room went dead silent, all eyes shifting to whatever this was.

Luke's voice was a low hum, smooth and deadly. "Didn't think you had the guts to show your face here."

His voice sliced through me, and I caught myself cataloguing the angle of his jaw. My fingers tightened around the edge of the tray. I forced my shoulders loose. Calm. This was a game. And I'd learned to play with the best. I met his gaze, steady and unflinching. "Looks as if someone's still nursing a grudge."

The shift was subtle—just a flicker of darkness in his eyes. But it was enough. I hit a nerve. Good.

He stepped closer, voice dropping just for me. "You don't belong here," he murmured, breath fanning across my cheek. "And I'll make sure everyone knows it."

Cedar and spice. The scent clung to my memory, bittersweet and cruel, dragging old warmth through new wounds.

I blinked up at him, slow. "Try me."

For a second, we just stared. Neither of us blinking. Neither of us moving. Then he scoffed and turned, his team following like well-trained dogs, peeling away just as the tension in the room snapped back into place.

My appetite had vanished. I dumped the tray and left, not looking back, even though I felt his gaze burn down my spine the whole way out.

I didn't slow down until I reached my locker. The metal clanged when I twisted the combo and yanked it open. My fingers shook, just a little. Just enough to piss me off.

He was harder now, colder, and sharper around the edges like someone had sanded down whatever softness he used to let me see. I hated wondering if I was the one who did that to him.

Then—out of nowhere—a body fell against the lockers.

"Girl, I heard you were back. Why didn't you call?"

Avery. Leaning against the locker next to mine like nothing had changed. Same confident smirk. Same cascade of honey-blonde waves. Same cornflower-blue eyes that missed nothing.

Relief punched the breath out of me. I hadn't realized how badly I needed an ally until she showed up, a lifeline. "I didn't exactly have a going-away party." I grabbed a notebook I needed for my next class. "Didn't think you would want anything to do with a vanishing act."

She scoffed. "Please. This is Blackwood. You gave the school a trust fund worth of drama. I eat that shit for breakfast." She looked me over. "You're lucky I like ghosts."

I smiled—small, real. "You're the first familiar face that hasn't tried to gut me. Why is that?"

"That's because I'm not stupid." She leaned in. "You'll tell me when you're ready, and I already witnessed the welcome wagon the guys gave you. Besides, I remember who you were." Her voice softened. "And I remember who you were with."

My stomach flipped. I shut my locker a little harder than necessary. "So does everyone else."

"You dated a King." She shrugged. "No one forgets a scandal of that magnitude. Least of all Elise."

Of course. I exhaled. "I used to run in their circle. Now I'm barely orbiting the planet."

Avery laughed, full and unbothered. "Coming in from the wrong side of the tracks, huh?"

Her tone was teasing, but her eyes were steady. Kind. She wasn't mocking me. She was marking the line I'd crossed. Power was currency in Blackwood. And I'd overstepped.

"You good with that?" she asked.

"I have to be."

She bumped her shoulder into mine. "Good. Because I hate fake people. And you coming back? You just made things a hell of a lot more fun."

We pushed off the lockers, weaving through the crush of students. People still stared. Still whispered.

Avery leaned closer. "Word of warning. Elise is already circling."

I'd caught that. "She never liked me."

"She tolerated you when you were Luke's. Then, she hadn't stood a chance. Funny that she thinks she has one now. It makes you competition."

I snorted. "I'm not competing."

"Doesn't matter. In her eyes? You walked back into *her* kingdom."

I arched a brow. "And Luke?"

Avery sighed. "Still untouchable. Still angry. Still acts like he's above it all." She paused. "But he saw you this morning. And trust me—it shook him."

I nodded once. The memory of that muscle jumping in his jaw came swift on the heels of her words. "Good."

Her gaze flicked over me. "Careful. Elise might run the socials, but Luke controls the oxygen. When they both target the same person?"

"I become the battlefield."

"Exactly."

We stopped outside the classroom. Avery looked at me, a flicker of something serious threading through the teasing. "Don't let her shrink you. You used to walk these halls like you owned them. You want back in? Take it. And, Mila?" Her hand briefly rested on my arm. "It's good to have you back."

I didn't say thank you. I didn't need to. Because in that moment, for the first time today, I wasn't completely alone.

Later during the day, we ended up in the same art class, one of the few places that still felt like mine. She sat at the station beside me, muttering about how she could barely sketch a stick figure. I rolled my eyes, pulled out my sketchbook, and let the rest of the world fade.

The air in the studio always smelled of dusty graphite, earthy oil paints, and the pungent bite of turpentine. Chalk dust clung to the floor. Sunlight poured through the tall windows, bouncing off metal stools and wide-plank hardwood. It wasn't fancy, but it was sacred. A place where everything else faded.

Our current project was a portrait series—faces, expressions, the little betrayals written across them.

Avery slouched two stools over with a graphite pencil in her mouth and a sketchpad she clearly hadn't opened. She looked up as I slid into my seat and offered a two-fingered salute, her grin easy. "Let's pretend I know what I'm doing."

I smirked. "Fake it till you make it."

"Fake it till they pass me so I never have to take this elective again," she muttered, flipping her sketchpad upside down like the pencil lines might rearrange themselves.

I dropped my bag, pulled out my sketchbook, and braced myself. The spine was peeling, its edges frayed. The cover was battered, marked with smudges of charcoal and the faded remnants of a coffee stain.

I flipped through slowly.

A sparring match from the gym below the apartment we lived in last year. Muscle, sweat, rage in motion. A guy with a split lip frozen mid-swing, the blur of gloves I'd rendered with fast, loose lines. Shading where the overhead light cast harsh shadows across his spine.

Then another page—waves crashing against the shore, gulls caught mid-flight. Feet in the foreground, mine, half-submerged as a wave receded. I'd drawn the moment between stillness and pull, how the ocean always felt hungry for something from you.

"Damn," Avery muttered, leaning over. "I've always envied your talent."

I shrugged. "Drawing helps me make sense of things, that's all."

"Should I be concerned if my sketch of this apple looks like a lumpy kidney?" she asked, rotating her paper for me to see.

I choked on a laugh. "First of all, it's upside down."

She blinked. "Oh. That explains nothing, but thank you."

I nudged her with my elbow then turned a few more pages.

Luke. Dozens of sketches of him, scattered like confessions. Profiles. Frontal angles. Full-body shots on the ice. I'd drawn his smirk once—crooked and smug, as if he knew something you didn't. His eyes more than once. The way he leaned on one foot, the way he always looked like he was moving even when he was still.

And always, his jaw. It was my favorite part to sketch. Clean, defined, and carved from intent. I'd shaded it so many times the graphite had rubbed off on the opposite page.

I paused. Then turned to a blank sheet.

This Luke was different. The softness I used to know had been carved out, replaced with angles and armor. His silence didn't just guard him now—it warned everyone else. Even the way he looked at me felt foreign. Like I was a threat. Or worse, a regret.

Even his eyes were colder now—still blue, still beautiful, but no longer forgiving. His hair was slightly longer at the top, his posture more rigid. I sketched the angle of his shoulders first— broader than before. The slope of his neck. The tension in his jawline. I added the shadows under his cheekbones, the set of his mouth that rarely relaxed anymore.

My pencil scratched out the truth in strokes and smears. Smudged the edge of his jaw with my thumb. Used the side of the graphite stick to deepen the hollows of his throat. Layered crosshatching over the collar of his shirt, remembering how he looked that morning in the cafeteria—eyes blazing, a warning flare.

I used the eraser to pull out a highlight in his lower lip. Another above his brow. I was chasing light and edge and all the things I would never be able to say.

Around me, students murmured, chairs scraped, the teacher droned on about structure and line weight. None of it mattered. I was buried in the lines of a guy who hated me, who still looked at me, unable to decide whether to destroy or protect.

I didn't even realize I was breathing easier until I looked down and saw the page nearly finished. Even if nothing else made sense, this did. This was mine. He used to be too.

That night, at home, I checked the school's tagged stories on Instagram. There it was. A looped video of Luke on the ice.

Scoring the game-winning goal. The crowd exploded. Avery was there, cheering on the sidelines. And I—just like I'd been for the past year—was the ghost. Still watching from the edge. Still missing from the picture.

CHAPTER FOUR

LUKE

I was built for this. The pre-game silence. The slight weight of protective gear strapped tight to my shoulders. The hum of fluorescent lights buzzing overhead, a countdown to war. In here, before the blood and ice and violence, I was steel. Calm. Locked in. Nothing else existed.

Not my family. Not the dynasty pressuring me to carry their legacy on my back. Not the whispers about who I used to be before I was crowned captain. Not the girl who vanished in the dead of night and left a crater in her wake.

Not today. Today was Crestview. Our oldest rival. The kind of game that set the tone for the entire season. And I was ready to detonate.

The guys gave me space. They always did when I got this way. They thought I was just in the zone—clinical, methodical, ruthless. Focused.

Theo cracked jokes in the corner, tearing an energy bar open with his teeth. Chase was pacing, hyped and twitchy. Jax sat near me, lacing his skates with that quiet, dangerous intensity that matched mine more than anyone else's. He didn't speak. He didn't have to.

I didn't look up. Just tightened my grip on the hockey stick between my knees, rolling my shoulders to shake off the last of whatever wasn't game-related.

But it was still there. In the back of my head—Mila. The earthquake beneath the surface I hadn't prepared for. The fault line I'd forgotten could still split me wide open.

She shook my world. But that didn't matter now. Because when everything else failed, I came back to the one thing I could count on. The ice. The game. The violence that asked for nothing but instinct and grit.

Not love. Not loyalty. Just blood, breath, and blades. And tonight? I was ready to burn.

My brother had texted me an hour before warm-ups. *You've got this.* Followed by a picture of him and his fiancée Claire at some business dinner, perfectly polished.

I didn't respond.

Drew was back in the fold now. Wearing ties. Playing house with the girl who'd saved his reputation. Pretending like he'd never fallen. But I remembered the nights he hadn't come home. The headlines our father had to bury. The glassy eyes and empty bottles.

The way he looked at me now—as if he wanted to believe I had it all under control, but he wasn't sure. He, most of all, knew the pressure our father put on us, and when he was counted out, the mantle had settled on my shoulders. It still rested there despite how he'd returned and stepped up. Our father didn't like unknowns, chances that weren't a sure thing—and Drew had, for a while, looked like one. Dad still treated him that way, and it pissed me off. I didn't understand how he could partially dismiss his oldest son.

Drew had cornered me in the kitchen before I left. Tie loosened, phone in one hand, the other braced on the counter. "You good?" His eyes searched too long. "Because if something's off— I can help. I've got your back."

I lied the way we all did. A short shrug, eyes steady. "I'm good."

His mouth had pressed flat, as if he'd wanted to say more but swallowed it.

I was the last one out of the locker room. The sound of my skate guards on concrete echoed down the tunnel, counting down each step toward the rink.

The air hit colder when I stepped onto the ice. The arena was packed—Blackwood Academy black and silver everywhere, chants vibrating against the plexiglass.

And then there she was. Not Mila. Avery. Dead center behind the bench, palms flat on the plexiglass, mouth already moving. Probably yelling at Chase. Probably loving every second of it. The seat beside her was empty. It used to be Mila's.

She'd sit with her legs folded, hoodie pulled halfway up over her hair, clutching a coffee, as if it could shield her from the cold she hated. I'd look over during breaks and found her watching me—not the game, *me*—as though she were memorizing every second.

And now she was gone. Still not here. But I felt her, a phantom limb. A song that used to play on repeat in the back of my head until I forgot how to stop humming it.

Coach called the first line. I didn't hesitate. Didn't think. I hit the ice and chased the puck as if it owed me something.

Crestview's forward made a lazy attempt at a cross-check near the blue line. I answered with a hit that rattled his bones. He dropped like a stone, stick sliding across the ice.

The crowd exploded. The ref's whistle came late—an afterthought. I didn't stop. Didn't blink. Just skated away while the trainers rushed the ice.

Back on the bench, Jax muttered, "Jesus."

Theo elbowed him. "He's in a mood."

I glanced down the bench and locked eyes with Logan—his

gaze laced with silent, bone-deep loathing. What the fuck was that about? For the moment, I dismissed it.

Chase just watched me, brow low.

I sat down and breathed deeply.

Avery slapped her palms against the glass again, grinning wide. But her eyes flicked to the empty seat beside her. Just for a second.

And that was when I knew. Mila would come. Maybe not tonight. Maybe not the next game. But she would show. She always had. And when she did, I would be ready. Because this wasn't over. Not even close.

<hr>

My father didn't call. He summoned.

One text from his assistant, and I was leaving the rink immediately after the game, still smelling like ice and sweat, to stand in the corner office of King Enterprises. Floor-to-ceiling glass framed the Blackwood skyline like a trophy case. Most of those buildings? Ours.

Grant King didn't look up from the folder in front of him. "You're late."

I dropped into the chair across from his desk. "I was at my game."

His gaze finally lifted—cold, assessing. "Sports are fine, but don't mistake it for a future. Hockey is a window, Luke. You need to start thinking about what happens when it closes."

This was nothing new. He'd been grooming me for the summer internship since I could drive. Made it sound as though it were an honor. A rite of passage. The truth? It was just another leash. I'd never quite forgiven him for how easily he'd written Drew off when he fell—alcohol, drugs, the spiral everyone witnessed but no one stopped. Dad had been pissed about the stain on the family name, not the fact his oldest son was drowning. That had been left to Claire and me to fix.

"Dunn Industries made an offer on the Bayview property this morning," he went on. "We can't let them get their hands on it."

I frowned. "It's just a hotel." He'd been looping me into deals like this for years, shaping me into whatever version of me he wanted sitting in this office one day.

"It's leverage," he corrected, leaning back in his chair. "If Dunn controls that block, it pushes us out of the harbor district. And if we lose that, we lose control of a lot more than you understand right now."

I didn't miss the way he glanced at the closed side door—Lorne's. The partner who handled the "messy" parts of the business. I'd learned early that whatever went on in those meetings wasn't for me to hear.

And that was the thing about my father—business talk was never *just* business. So when he shifted gears, I knew it was a setup.

"You'll be polite to Elise Dunn," he added smoothly, as if it were just another line item on a spreadsheet. "Keep her close. If Charles Dunn wants a working relationship, we give him the illusion of one. And another thing—you'll stay away from distractions," he said, tone sharp enough to cut. "I hear Mila Callahan is back."

My pulse jumped, but I kept my voice flat. "And?"

"And you would be smart to remember why she left. Your mother and I warned you about her. That family is trouble. Always has been."

The flash of the necklace burned in my mind—finding it in my hockey bag like the ultimate fuck you parting gift. I stood, adjusting the strap of my duffel. "Anything else?"

"Yes. Family is what matters. Protecting it comes before everything."

I met his stare. "Sure. Family first." What I didn't say was that family was the only thing that could cut you the deepest. And some wounds never stopped bleeding.

35

CHAPTER FIVE

MILA

The moment I stepped into the hallway the next day, the air was so thick with tension, I nearly choked on it. Heads turned, whispers rippled past me, curling upward the way cigarette smoke did. I slowed, senses spiraling. Something was wrong.

Clusters of girls—Elise's crew—lined the lockers ahead. They parted, backs stiffening, allowing her to glide forward first. A black leather jacket, heels clicking against tile, designer bag swinging low. Triumph shadowed her eyes. A smile curved her lips, a fuse freshly lit.

I froze by my locker, stomach twisting as I saw *Trash* scrawled across the metal in jagged black marker. The ink dripped, bleeding into the surface, part watercolor gone wrong, part open wound. My chest clenched, but I refused to wince.

One thing was for sure, I didn't dress the same. Jeans, a gray vintage fitted T-shirt, and beat-up sneakers. I liked what I wore, but Mom and I had never wasted cash on designer brands when we could find cool knockoffs or other styles. Did I want to look like Elise? I let my gaze travel the length of her. Nope. Not even a little. If I wanted to wear designer clothes someday, I would for me, but never to fit in. I wasn't built that way.

Elise stopped two lockers down, arms folded. The corners of her lips twitched with amusement.

I snorted. She thought defacing my locker would crack me. She didn't know. I'd survived worse.

A year ago, my mom and I had landed in East LA—squatting in neighborhoods where gang members ruled the hallways, not princesses in designer jackets. I traded heels for beaten sneakers and learned to fight on my feet. Edwardo, the boxing instructor who let us crash in the apartment above the gym, taught me how to throw punches—and how to take them. He was divorced, had a daughter who lived in another state, and he took me under his wing as though I was his own.

Elise sneered. "Looks like someone doesn't want you here."

Tori, her sidekick, leaned in. Her whispered *"charity case"* cut through the air. Elise laughed—teeth bright and sharp. Nina brought up the rear and shoulder-checked me hard enough to jolt me.

I didn't flinch. A shoulder-check? Child's play. I let a smirk curl. My eyes hardened.

Elise watched, waiting for me to shrink. I met her gaze. "That the best you've got?"

Her smirk faltered—before she recovered, flicked her jet-black hair, and said, "Oh, sweetheart, this is just the beginning."

I rolled my eyes and yanked open the locker with more force than necessary. If she thought a little vandalism would scare me, she would never survive a battlefield.

By the time lunch rolled around, it felt like I had walked into an arena where I was the main show. Conversations stilled as I stepped in. Every table shifted, predatory—sharks circling fresh blood. It was getting old, but I had to deal.

At the center sat Luke, framed by his teammates—Jax, Chase, Theo. He leaned into the group, arms crossed, head tilted slightly. Untouchable. Unbothered. But the moment our eyes met, everything shifted. Hurt flickered in his gaze. Suspicion. Regret. Then *poof*—all of it buried under layers of polished apathy.

Before I could even center myself, a tray of steaming pasta splattered onto my chest. Red sauce splotched my shirt. Elise's bloodred nails still gripped the edge of the tray as she smirked.

"Well, don't you look like a public service announcement," she said, loud enough for half the cafeteria to hear. "Some people need a little seasoning."

I swallowed my discomfort. But I refused to let her see me squirm. "Fuck off, Elise." Anger rolled through me, but it wasn't fully directed at her. She wasn't even worthy of being on my radar.

The first school we ran to after leaving Blackwood was in the worst part of LA—East LA. Real gang turf wars, real violence. I'd seen knives, shivs, bodies dropped behind taco trucks. I survived that. There was no way a cafeteria stunt scared me. It was uncomfortable, unwanted, but survivable and far from the end of the world.

My tray, still in my hands, tilted, slipping from my grip, and a malicious grin curved my mouth as I let it fall. The tray hit with a clang. Chili launched like shrapnel—most notably onto Elise's pristine, knee-high Balenciaga boots. White. Of course they were white.

Her shriek knifed through the room. "Are you fucking serious?" She looked down at her boots, staring at them as if they were casualties in a fight she hadn't signed up for. Sauce slid down the supple leather, pooling near the heel. A bean clung to the toe. Her nostrils flared. "These cost more than your life."

I didn't even flinch. But when her head snapped toward Luke—eyes wide, pleading, expecting him to unleash hell on her behalf—something in me snapped.

The look she gave him wasn't just panic. It was possessive. Expectant. As if he was hers. Like I never existed.

I didn't hesitate. Stalking across the room, red sauce and defiance dripping in my wake, I didn't stop until I made it to *his* table.

"Enjoying the show?" I asked, loud enough to hush the room.

Luke's jaw ticked. He didn't blink. "I don't know what you're talking about."

I laughed, low and humorless. "Right. Cowardly games. Whispered threats." And because I was furious, I lobbed a blow beneath the belt. "Funny how the prince of Blackwood turned into his father's puppet."

I spat it at him, daring him to take it. And with every eye in the room on us, I sent the message: I'm not afraid.

Luke's eyes darkened—the only reaction he gave—and that was enough.

Theo cleared his throat behind me. "Dude."

All eyes flicked between him and Elise.

Luke didn't answer Theo. He didn't even blink. And that silence said more than any words.

Fine, he wasn't going to own up? Whatever. I let my gaze cut to Elise. Funny—she wasn't directly at his side, no matter how hard she pretended she was. She had underestimated me. And I never forgot who drew first blood.

I couldn't stay. My chest was tight, and an outraged tremor shook my hands. I abandoned my tray where I left it, hightailed it out of the cafeteria, and headed to the bathroom.

I locked the bathroom door behind me, the echo a little too final. My hand still trembled from Elise's tray smashing into my chest, but it wasn't her I was spiraling about. Not really.

From my bag, I pulled out my backup shirt—a tight white tee. I didn't choose it to blend in but to be seen. Once on, I studied myself in the mirror. It hugged my body like a second skin, the faint outline of my bra visible beneath, my breasts strained against the fabric. My gray eyes were smoky, filled with fire. Fury lit me from the inside out. *Let them come at me.*

I yanked out my phone. My thumb hovered for a moment before tapping the contact I swore I wouldn't. It rang twice.

"Mila?" My mom's voice slid through as if she'd been holding her breath all day.

I leaned back against the cool tile wall, stared at the flickering light overhead. "Why are we really back here?" I needed to know the day-in, day-out torture was worth it.

A pause. Long enough to feel like an answer. "You know why. Blackwood Academy opens doors. You graduate from there, you get into whatever college you want. And this job will give us financial security. That was the deal."

"Bullshit," I said quietly. "That was the bait. What's the hook?"

I could hear her exhale. A chair scraping in the background. Papers shifting.

"We agreed to a clean slate. I thought we could make it work —one year. Just enough for you to finish strong and move on."

I didn't believe her. It was the same canned answer she gave me before. It hurt. We'd always been a team. She told me her plans, her secrets, and I'd shared mine. But not now. From the moment she said we were moving back, she'd been a vault.

Hanging up, I pushed the unhelpful conversation with my mom aside, wishing it could've given me answers, or at the very least, helped take my mind off today's latest shit show.

I didn't want to care about any of it, especially Luke. But the thing about pretending not to care? It was harder when I remembered the last time he looked at me like he meant it. And when the thought hit, the memory rolled through my mind like a tidal wave I had no hopes of fighting.

The roof of the arena still radiated warmth from the sun, even though the night air had cooled. I lay back on the worn plaid blanket, spine against steel, eyes lost in the kind of sky you only got in these places—far from city lights, where stars punched through the dark like tiny, stubborn rebellions.

Luke lay beside me, one arm bent under his head, the other stretched just enough that our hands brushed, knuckles ghosting against one another in lazy intervals. We hadn't spoken in minutes. We didn't need to.

Everything about tonight was quiet—our breath, the flick of wind curling around the building's edge, the distant hum of the rooftop lights blinking behind us. It was the kind of quiet that filled you up and hollowed you out all at once.

Then it streaked across the sky. A shooting star. It burned silver and then was gone in a breath, but I felt it like an earthquake in my chest.

Luke turned his head toward me. "Did you see that?"

"Hard to miss." I smiled, but my eyes stayed on the trail it left behind, already fading. "Quick, make a wish."

He huffed a low breath. "You believe in that stuff?"

"Doesn't matter," I said. "Say it anyway."

He didn't speak right away. Just stared upward like the stars had answers he didn't know how to ask for. Then: "Freedom."

The word was simple. But his voice made it anything but.

I turned my head then. Studied the sharp lines of his jaw, the way his mouth pressed into a quiet frown. "From what?"

He didn't look at me. "All of it. My name. The company. The weight I didn't choose but can't seem to drop." He finally glanced over. "It's as if I'm always holding my breath for a life that isn't mine. Just once, I want to exhale."

The ache in my chest deepened. I swallowed, voice tight. "I wish I had that kind of courage."

His brow furrowed. "You do."

"No." I turned back to the sky, stars swimming in my vision. "I wish I trusted myself enough to go after what I really want. That art wasn't just some reckless dream to my mom. That money didn't have its claws in everything. That I could believe my talent mattered more than making rent or playing it safe."

He didn't interrupt, just listened, the way he always did when I cracked myself open, piece by piece. Things were different with him—he was the only person I had truly let in to see all of me. And it felt like I was the same for him.

"I wish wanting something didn't feel like betrayal."

My throat thickened. "I want to believe it's okay to want more. Not just survival. But something that's *mine*."

There was a rustle beside me, and then his hand slid into mine. No words. Just a tether.

And in that moment, under a sky painted with a thousand silent promises, I believed him. I believed that we could both choose something bigger than our bloodlines. That hockey could be his oxygen. That art could be mine. That we were two people caught in a world too heavy—and we were somehow holding each other up.

I rolled onto my side and pressed my lips to his. Soft. Slow. The kind of kiss that didn't just say *I want you*. It said *I see you*. It said *me too*.

He smiled against my mouth. "Make your wish."

"I already did," I whispered.

A few weeks later, in the locker room after morning warm-ups, I waited until everyone cleared out. Luke's bag sat in the corner, unzipped, his gear already half-spilling out like always.

I reached around my neck and unclasped it—the delicate white-gold chain he'd given me after that one night under the stars, the same one I never took off. A single star charm dangled from the center, catching the light like it remembered that night too.

I slipped it into the small zippered pouch on the inside flap of his bag. No note. No big moment. Just a quiet offering. I didn't want him to know right away. I wanted him to find it later. After the game. When he needed a reminder of what we'd promised each other in the dark.

———

Luke

The cafeteria buzzed long after Mila had walked away. I didn't say a word. Didn't defend myself. Didn't stop her. I just stood there. Let her accuse me. Let her tear into me—and maybe she had every right to.

"You good, man?" Theo nudged my shoulder as the team filtered out of the cafeteria.

"Fine."

He didn't believe me. "You didn't say a damn thing."

I shrugged. "Didn't seem worth it."

Jax scoffed behind me. "Looked like she hit a nerve."

"Shut up." I fought the urge to spin around and tear into Elise. But that wasn't me in this situation. Not anymore. Not in front of everyone when I couldn't back Mila. Not after what she'd done—or why she'd left. And especially after my father's mandate.

The room drained of people. Only the four of us remained, the space feeling hollow. They shut up—not because they respected me but because they knew what I was capable of.

And because they knew what their own families were tied to. Chase's dad worked closely with mine. Jax's father handled contracts through Lorne—the cleaner behind King Enterprises' more "strategic" moves. If anyone understood what it meant to have your hands tied by blood and legacy, it was them.

But I felt it. Cracks spreading. Mila knew my weakness. She'd tapped it. And my father? My brother? That looming empire? It was a twisted web I'd been crawling through without warning.

I locked eyes with Chase. His look said it all—he saw the fracture forming beneath the wall I'd erected. He heard the silent echo between Mila's words and my silence.

"Elise's next move?" he asked quietly. "Are you going to back her?"

I didn't answer. Because no one could know what this war was doing to me. Not yet.

CHAPTER SIX

LUKE

Sunlight streamed into our kitchen, taunting me—making everything look warmer than it felt. I slid onto a stool at the sleek marble island, ignoring the green smoothie Mom had left behind before dashing off to tennis or brunch or whatever social camouflage she wore that day. Coffee mattered more this morning.

Drew leaned against the counter across from me in a crisp button-down, sipping the coffee I wanted. Claire, his fiancée, flipped through her tablet, picking at fruit with delicate precision. They looked… staged.

"Morning, bro." He looked up from his phone with a grin that hovered somewhere between smug and too rehearsed. "You look like hell."

I grunted. "Didn't sleep."

He raised an eyebrow. "You've got bags under your eyes darker than your jersey. Are you skipping lifting or just prioritizing brooding?"

Claire glanced up, her voice soft but too curious to be casual. "He's probably just adjusting to school again." Her brown eyes flicked to mine. "I saw Mila Callahan's mom in town. Guess Mila is back. That must've been... a surprise?"

I forced the tension from my jaw. "Didn't expect her back."

Claire's fork hovered mid-air. "I always liked her. Not sure why she left so suddenly, but she seemed... interesting."

"She was," Drew said, sharper than expected. "But nobody disappears without reason. Especially not her mom. They didn't just leave—they vanished. That kind of thing leaves a mark."

I shrugged. "It's high school. Not a soap opera."

His tone darkened. "Just don't let her throw you off. You've got college coming up. Dad's under enough pressure already with Dunn Industries snapping at our heels, and we could use you stepping up at the company—sooner rather than later."

I stood, the chair scraping back across the hardwood. "Don't worry. I've got it handled."

Claire's gaze lingered on me, too quiet now. Drew didn't push further. But the mention of pressure... it crawled under my skin. Something had been simmering all summer. Reports, late-night calls, meetings that turned into arguments. The calm before the storm wasn't calm at all. It was waiting to detonate.

I stormed out of the house, the door slamming behind me. Backpack slung over my shoulder, I launched into the SUV, peeled down the driveway, and flew toward school, tires screeching into the front row of the student lot. My usual spot was still empty.

Chase, Jax, and Theo waited by their vehicles. They saw my expression and didn't bother with jokes.

"Some bullshit rumor's flying around," Theo said as I passed.

"Not now," I snapped.

But even as I shoved the door open and walked into school, I could feel it—the shift. The glances. The cut-off conversations. My name surfacing in tones too low to catch.

The King name usually carried reverence, not questions. I shouldn't care. It wasn't what mattered to me, or the future I wanted, but fuck it. I did care. And it echoed Drew's shitty mood.

Two girls near a locker—one of them I recognized from honors physics—were whispering.

"My dad works at Dunn. Said the VP at King Enterprises, Langley or some name like that, was about to go public with something. Then he just… vanished. I guess he got fired and was forced out of town."

"So what? That's old news. And besides, it's King. They still own everything."

"Not if layoffs happen. Logan's dad—he's out. No warning."

I stopped cold. They were facts. I knew because I'd heard similar when I shouldn't have. These weren't just hallway lies. That was blood in the water.

I ducked down a side hall to breathe, to think. The walls felt too close. My last name, usually my armor, now felt like a target painted on my back.

And then I saw her—Mila. By her locker. Talking low with two students I didn't recognize. She leaned in. Her eyes lit with something too close to determination. I moved toward her before I even knew what I was doing. She looked up. Her expression didn't change, didn't soften.

"Something interesting?" I asked, voice edged in steel.

The other girls scattered as she crossed her arms. "You tell me."

I stepped closer. "Rumors are swirling. You just got back, and suddenly shit's starting up again. Kind of like when you left the last time too."

Her chin lifted. "Funny—because from what I'm hearing, it's your father who's the common denominator."

A muscle twitched in my jaw. She had no clue what she was stirring up. But I did. Emergency board meetings. One of the exec's car totaled in a back-road accident three towns over. My dad's phone lighting up, his face gray as concrete when he finally emerged from his office that night. My mother disappearing for days at a time, always on the move but saying little.

I stepped into her space. "Stay out of it. Or you'll find yourself in a situation you can't walk away from."

She didn't move. Just stared back like I was some puzzle she'd already solved.

"I'm just following a thread," she said.

"Walk away, Mila."

Her slate-gray eyes with emerald flecks stayed locked on mine.

And for the first time in a long time, I felt something shift inside me—an unease that had nothing to do with her and everything to do with what I couldn't see coming. Because this wasn't just about us. It was about something bigger.

A conversation from the night before echoed in my skull. I'd just gotten home from the arena. Gear slung over my shoulder. I was headed upstairs when I paused outside Dad's office. The door wasn't shut all the way. Mom's voice—brittle, clipped—cut through the quiet.

"Lorne said it was handled. That nothing would trace back to us."

A pause. Then Dad: "It better not. If that audit gets reopened—"

"It was a mistake," Mom snapped. "You trusted him too much."

"We didn't have a choice."

"You always have a choice. You just don't like the ones that cost you."

Silence hung heavy before Mom's voice turned acerbic. "Adriana Callahan is back. Darren's girl. Maybe this time something can be done about what she took."

I stepped back, heart hammering. Darren Langley's girl. Mila's mom. And that meant Mila would also be in the crosshairs of whatever disaster was coming.

Her mom had worked for us. Or maybe *with* us. Hard to tell with people like my father. Whatever role she'd played, she'd left under a cloud. And suddenly, Mila wasn't just a ghost from my past. She was a threat.

I snapped back to the present. Mila's too-observant eyes glued to the emotions probably visible in mine. Fuck. I needed to get the hell out of there. She would be in all my classes starting today, but I needed to think, and I wasn't going to be able to do that here. So, I left—pushed open the school's main door, walked outside, and got in my SUV.

I went to the one place that was mine—the arena, and I hit the ice. I skated until my lungs burned and my body screamed for oxygen. Until I couldn't tell the difference between rage and panic. Every slap of the puck into the net was a shout I didn't let out. Every rotation a countdown to detonation.

Mila didn't know what she was stepping into. But I did. Her mom was already marked. And if she kept digging, she'd end up a casualty. Not because she was guilty. Because people in power didn't like questions. And I couldn't save her. Not if she didn't want to be saved.

I finished up, stepped out of the rink and into the locker room. Practice wasn't for a few hours. It was lunch, and I was debating whether to finish out the school day or just go home.

The echo of my footsteps was the only sound. I should've let it go with Mila earlier. Walked away. She was always so damn good at getting under my skin—knowing exactly which nerve to press like it was hers to own.

I pulled off my jersey, trying to let the burn in my lungs quiet the fire in my chest. But it didn't work. Not when the memory of her lingered—those captivating eyes, that unwavering stare, the defiance that used to come with a laugh and my mouth on hers in the backseat of my SUV. Back when we still believed we could outrun everything that chased us.

And then she walked into the locker room.

I blinked, thinking I'd imagined her. But there she was—Mila. Just inside the door, a bold line of tension held in her frame like she dared me to tell her to leave.

"Locker rooms are off-limits." I dragged the towel over my head. "Even for girls who think they're invincible."

She folded her arms. "They didn't use to be. Not with us."

I turned toward her, jaw tight even as a dozen images bombarded me of us together in this locker room. Her soft skin against mine. Her breathy moan haunting me until I wanted to throw something. "They are now. You keep throwing yourself into places you don't belong."

"Funny. I was about to say the same to you."

Silence stretched between us.

"Why now?" I asked finally, voice low. "Why come back?"

She hesitated. And that hesitation said more than any lie ever could. "I didn't have a choice."

"Bullshit. You always had a choice. You just didn't pick me."

She flinched, the movement almost too small to catch. Her swallow was audible.

"You think I wanted to leave?" she whispered.

I stepped closer. "You didn't even say goodbye."

"Because I couldn't."

I reached out. Not to touch her—just to be close enough to feel it. That thrum. That impossible tether between us. "I searched for you. For months."

"I know."

"Then why lie?"

She met my gaze, fire clashing with guilt. "Because it was the only way to protect us both."

She was right. The only way to protect her could very well be to stay far away from her. And I would try, starting now.

So I brushed past her, left her behind, and shoved open the door to exit the locker room. Then I was outside, sweat cooling against my skin, when a black SUV rolled to a stop near the curb. Window down. Tinted glass. Too smooth to be a coincidence.

"Luke," a familiar voice said.

Lorne.

I stared at the car for a second too long before climbing in. The inside smelled like leather and control. Lorne didn't look up right away, just tapped something on a sleek tablet, casual as hell. When he finally glanced over, his smile was polished steel. Dark eyes holding promises no one wanted to know, his presence filled the car with power, despite the caramel-colored highlights and custom-tailored suit that pretended to civilize the brutal nature underneath.

"You're making waves this season."

We'd had one game. But I knew scouts were watching. What I didn't know was why Lorne was.

"Coaches are noticing."

I didn't answer.

"But it's not just performance anymore." He leaned in, resting his elbow on the armrest. "Perception matters. And lately, the whispers… they're loud. About your father, the business, and a woman who came back to town who never should have."

I stiffened. Letting Lorne into your head in any capacity wasn't healthy. I couldn't even hint that Mila or her mom mattered. Not if I wanted to buy time to see if there was anything I could do. If I even wanted to, I still wasn't sure. "Let them talk."

Lorne's smile thinned. "You sound like your dad used to. Before the pressure chipped away at his judgment."

I looked at him fully. "Are you saying I'm making a mistake?" This man was my father's business partner and someone who was a part of my family since I could remember, but there was something dangerous about him we all took note of—even if he was supposedly on our side. None of us wanted to imagine him on the other side.

"I'm saying strong men don't let emotion cloud their control. Don't let the past dictate their future."

He was talking about Mila. Fuck. "I'm not my dad."

"No." He paused. "You're still becoming someone."

He handed me a folded piece of paper. I recognized the logo even before I unfolded it. One of our silent partners.

"Just keep your head clear. Eyes forward."

When I stepped out of the car and opened the paper, my stomach dropped. It wasn't just a development property. It was the boardwalk art studio Dad had sworn we would protect. But it was listed for sale. Lorne's name was at the bottom. And suddenly, everything I thought I knew was the first crack before the avalanche.

CHAPTER SEVEN

MILA

The hallway was quiet. I'd just come from the office where the secretary informed me that my class schedule had been rearranged. I should've known. It was only a matter of time before Luke stepped in and did something. This was his chess move. I knew, without even going to my first class of the day, that I would find him and the rest of the guys in it. Maybe even Avery—I hoped she would be there as a buffer against them.

Morning light filtered through the windows, and my backpack tugged at my shoulder as I paused to count the lockers until mine. That was when I saw Elise.

Across the hallway, her silhouette punched through the stillness. She leaned back against a locker, arms folded, eyes narrowed. Around her, a couple of her minions hovered—smirks on their faces, phones out, waiting.

Logan Mitchel, one of the hockey players, slouched beside her, his smirk slick as oil. That was new. I didn't know much about him, but they looked chummy, and when he glanced at me—dark eyes gleaming, thin lips curled into a smug smile—my skin crawled. That reaction alone told me everything I needed. He was bad news. And his proximity to Elise made him worse.

Still, I squared my shoulders. I'd been through worse. A graffitied locker, a plate full of spaghetti smashed into me, and a thousand whispers. It was different than my last school. There, I excelled at keeping to the shadows, being invisible. The risk of drawing too much attention, of gaining the notice of the wrong crowd or even person, might mean a switchblade to the leg or a fight in the bathroom. Here, they used words as their weapons. I could easily play that game I wasn't afraid of what they threw at me. Because nothing they tried could ever hurt me. I would have to care for it to, and I didn't. They were a tiny blip on my radar.

I kept walking. She didn't wait.

"Look how far you've fallen," Elise called, voice loud enough to echo. The clack of lockers clicked closed behind her minions. "You think you can come back, make another play at Luke?"

My fingers tightened on my bag. I ignored her. She wasn't worth wasting air on. And if it was Luke she wanted—which clearly, she did—she could have him. He wasn't the same guy I'd fallen for. The hardness in his eyes, the chill emanating off him, told me more than enough. The worst-case scenario was probably already in play—he was becoming his father. *And it's my fault.*

She stepped forward, spine straight, chin tilted in practiced defiance. "That's cute. You really think you can walk back in and pretend you belong?"

Her followers burst into overloud laughter. Elise's nails dug into my shoulder, stopping me from walking away. I shrugged her off and rolled my eyes.

Then Avery appeared beside me and dropped her book bag with a thud. "Back off." Her voice a low growl.

Elise tucked a strand of her jet-black hair behind her ear while shifting her focus smoothly, expression oiled into sweetness. "Oh, look—Mila's sidekick decided to show up. You best watch your back, Avery." She smiled too wide. "Power's shifting, sweetheart. You might want to learn who's really running things."

My eyebrow rose, and I fought the urge to see if any of the guys were nearby, wondering what they would have to say to Elise's bold move. "That doesn't scare me."

"Once my brother hears, you'll be the one afraid," Avery promised Elise, her lips rearranging into a sneer. She flicked her long, wavy blond ponytail over her shoulder and met Elise's brown-eyed gaze.

"We'll see." Elise tipped her head toward the end of the hall. "They're watching." Her gaze locked on two figures by the trophy case—Luke's crew. "Luke is gonna have a choice soon, and you won't like his decision."

My gaze flew to the guys, wondering if they'd heard anything. But they couldn't have, or they would've come over. They set their gaze around us, mostly on Avery. Jax with folded arms. Theo clutching his phone, probably because he'd alerted Luke. Chase, silent, coiled. Avery's brother had become way more protective of her since I'd left. I couldn't help but wonder what had changed to cause him to act the way he was.

Avery's jaw was clenched, her arms crossed. Loyal as hell. I squared my shoulders and met Elise's smirk. "Good luck. I'll enjoy watching the guys remind you where you stand."

Elise laughed, as if admitting defeat would blow her mind. Around us, melting whispers rose, a tide pulling at the edges. Did she really think she could go up against them? Something flickered in her eyes before she turned, hair swishing, heels echoing back down the hall. Her entourage fell in line, triumphant and vicious.

Avery guided me to my locker. "You all right?" she whispered.

"Yeah." I continued to watch their retreat. "She's rattled, right? I wasn't."

Avery's eyes flicked back to the trophy case where the guys were, now complete with Luke. "It's not him she's worried about."

I wanted to laugh. Elise was a fool because she definitely should be worried about him.

Avery worried her lip, and I sighed, giving in to the need to reassure her. "I'm fine. Seriously. I don't give a shit about her games."

Avery studied me for a second before the tension eased, and her shoulders loosened. "Come on." She linked arms with me. "Let's get to class."

We rounded the corner. The murmurs followed. Behind us, I knew the guys watched. Let them. Whatever Elise had on them would soon be dissected, or maybe it already was. I glanced at Jax, then Luke, noting the calculating gleam that told me they were thinking, weighing just how and why the battlefield had changed.

By some miracle, I made it through all my classes without incident. Avery stuck close when we had any that were together. It was unfortunate that I didn't have more than one that the guys weren't in. But they weren't making moves. Not yet. When Avery had asked if I wanted to meet later in the library after school, I took her up on it. Even though I didn't want to remain here, going home was even less of a desire. The house was a dump, and Mom and I had this weirdness between us ever since we stepped foot in this stupid town.

The library felt colder than usual, even with the late afternoon sun spilling through the tall windows. I hovered near one of the long study tables, fingers drumming against the edge of my battered Calculus textbook. The same page had been open for ten minutes. I hadn't read a single problem. And how could I after that confrontation with Luke in the rink's locker room earlier? I'd wanted answers, but all the questions I would've asked burned away at the sight of him without a shirt on. Sweat had glistened, only highlighting how broad and cut he was. He'd always been athletic, gorgeous, and alluring. But now? He was downright irresistible. And untouchable. It made me ache in ways I couldn't admit.

Avery slid into the seat across from me, scattering my thoughts to the wind. Her ponytail was too perfect, and her face gave away nothing, but I could feel the shift in her vibe, as if something weighed on her.

"I know we brushed everything under the table—you leaving, all that. And I didn't ask you here to rehash because I didn't come to talk about the past," she said, voice flat as she dropped her bag beside her.

"Good." I flipped the page as if it mattered, almost relieved we were going to hash something out. "Because I wouldn't even know where to start."

Heavy silence fell between us. A few quiet conversations drifted over from another table. A chair creaked behind me.

"You always hated math," Avery finally said with a sigh, as if it annoyed her to admit she remembered.

"I still do," I muttered, glancing up again. Mom wished it was otherwise; math was her thing, not mine.

A ghost of a smirk tugged at her mouth before she wiped it away. "Then it's a good thing I'm a math goddess."

I arched a brow. "You mean aside from that one test sophomore year?"

"Oh my God. One time I bomb, and you never let me live it down."

"Math goddess, huh?" I deadpanned. "Bold title."

Another silence stretched, but this one felt... easier. Less jagged. And I breathed easier. Guess we weren't going to hash things out. I was okay with that too, so long as she decided she still wanted to be my friend—because I needed one.

"I didn't expect you to actually show up," I said after a beat, my voice softer than I meant it to be.

"I didn't expect you to actually come back," she fired. "But here we are."

"It's not like I had a choice," I muttered, regret swarming me until tears pricked my eyes. I blinked them back, spinning my pencil between tense fingers. "It wasn't that simple."

She studied me, blue eyes narrowed, unreadable. "It never is with you."

We dropped back into the textbook, the silence between us filled with soft page turns and half-mumbled notes. It was familiar—unsettlingly so, a friendship put in storage and shoved back into the light. Maybe it still meant something. Maybe I was stupid enough to hope it did.

A few problems later, Avery took a swig from her water bottle, and her voice changed—quieter now. Cautious.

"You're not the only one Elise is gunning for, you know." She shifted, her face tightening. "I didn't really want to get into this, but I feel like you should know. She's got it bad for you, and that's not good." She paused. "When you were gone last year, Rachel Lewinsky told some friends she liked Luke. Thought she had a shot."

I raised a brow. "Don't most girls think that here?"

Avery gave a shrug, but her expression didn't match the casualness. "Yeah, well... Elise overheard. She pretended to be Rachel's friend for weeks before she went full DEFCON 1. Pulled her close, made her feel like she finally belonged. Even set her up to accidentally run into Luke between classes, made it look like he might be interested. Then Elise twisted things, humiliated her in front of everyone. Bullied her hard. Told her to go kill herself."

My blood iced. "Wait—she actually said that?" That wasn't something to mess around with. Words had power. It wasn't possible to know if someone was on the ledge or not. Plenty of people faked being okay. One line like that could push them over.

Avery nodded. "Rachel tried. OD'd. Her mom found her before it was too late."

Silence cracked between us. My throat locked up. "Jesus."

"Yeah. Elise is a piece of work." Avery's eyes misted over. "But you want to know what happened to her?"

"I'm guessing nothing." Elise had money. Her dad ran Dunn Industries—one of the only companies in town that could rival King Enterprises.

"Not a damn thing. Rachel's family was offered hush money —and a threat. Either take it and move away, or stay and never work in this town again."

"Elise did that?"

"Her dad did. Protected her. Like always."

I studied Avery. The way her shoulders curled inward. "What did she do to you?"

Her breath hitched. Eyes wide. "Nothing really," she denied too fast. "Just... after you left, she harassed me. I didn't handle it well."

I reached across the table, covered her hand. "Aves. I'm so sorry. I would've reached out if I could. But my mom—there were reasons. I didn't even tell Luke."

She pulled her hand back. "It's okay. I mean it. But you can't tell anyone what I said."

"Not even your brother?"

"No." Her voice hardened. "Chase thinks it was some guy who messed with me. And yeah, he was pissed you bailed on us too."

That didn't sound right. The guys—they never would've let that go. "They would've pushed harder if they thought it was a guy."

"I stonewalled them. I didn't want them fighting my battles. Eventually, they stopped asking. But now Chase goes full attack dog on anyone who looks at me." She gave a dry laugh. "Might've been a mistake."

"You ever gonna tell him?"

She straightened. "No. I'm allowed to have secrets from my twin and his pack of wolves. Just... watch your back. Elise is vicious. And when it comes to Luke?"

I nodded. "She's pissed he's not looking at her."

"Exactly."

My pencil stilled mid-equation. Luke's name struck, hard enough to leave me reeling.

Avery noticed. Of course she did. "Whatever happened between you two? It left marks. On both of you."

I looked up slowly, meeting her gaze. "Yeah," I said. "It did." The kind that didn't fade. That burned new every time he looked at me like I was something he wanted to forget.

She didn't look away. Neither did I as the truth of the matter lay bare between us. I wasn't going to explain myself, and she wasn't asking me too. Her trust in me to let it lie was humbling.

"Come to the game with me."

I didn't even think, just—fuck no. "That's a hard pass, Aves."

Her lips twitched again at the old nickname. "Luke's on the ice. He and my brother can't do anything. No scenes. No bullshit. Jasmine and Margie will be there too."

"Is that supposed to mean something to me?" I wasn't friends with them. She knew that. I hadn't been friends with anyone other than her and the guys. But that all changed in one night when Mom and I left without goodbyes or an explanation.

She shrugged. "No. I supposed it doesn't. You never hung out with anyone except the guys or me. Still, I want you to come with. It'll be fun. And they're nice. They won't give you shit, promise."

The hockey games were a rush, but going there... "I don't know. Luke won't like that I'm there."

"Pffft. When has that ever stopped you from doing something?" Her brows rose in challenge. "Or are you not the same person I used to know?"

That hit harder than it should've. Not because it wasn't true. But because she was right. I didn't even know who the hell I was anymore since coming back here.

I tapped my pencil against hers, a smile slowly spreading across my face, so damn grateful she'd forgiven me and let me back in so easily. Too easily. It made me nervous. What kind of penance hadn't I paid yet? "Fine. I'll go, even if only to keep Chase off your back."

"Come on." Her phone pinged, and she rolled her eyes. The name was easy to read with her phone sitting face up on the table. Chase was checking in on her for the third time that night. "I love him, but I swear he still thinks I'm ten. Or maybe it's because I was a shell of my former self last year—he thought I would be the next Rachel. I promise you, I wasn't anywhere close to being on the ledge like that." She shrugged, brushing off the heavy topic. "He's a serious pain in my ass. I should just call him the vagina blocker."

I snorted a laugh then rolled my eyes as the only other person that remained in the library turned and glared before pushing up her glasses with her middle finger. With a shake of my head at the ridiculousness of it all, the last of the tension between my shoulders eased since the moment my old friend sat down across from me.

It was a bad idea, but when had that ever stopped me before? "I'll meet you there."

Avery shrieked, earning another glare from the bookworm a table over. We agreed on a time and then headed out. I needed to drop my books at home, grab a sandwich, and maybe wash my face. There was no way I was dressing differently, except to grab a hoodie if I was cold, which I would be. The jeans and T-shirt I had on blended in, the hoodie would even more so, and that was what I wanted.

An hour later, I stood inside the entrance of Blackwood's arena, a thousand misgivings running through my mind. The crowd was loud as Avery dragged me through the entrance anyway, her grip ironclad as she muttered about needing a wingwoman. The noise of the crowd swelled enough to crawl under my skin in an itchy sort of way. I trailed behind her through the aisles and to my dawning horror, the front seats behind the box.

I should have known she would sit there. It was the section we used to lay claim to. As we arrived at the end of the aisle, the hockey team filed onto the bench in front of us, all bulk and blades.

Avery's friend Jasmine waved us over. I kept my gaze straight ahead, refusing to look through the plexiglass to my left. It was the only thing that separated us and the team, specifically Luke and the rest of his crew. The hair on the back of my neck rose from the sensation of being watched.

I took measured breaths then eased into the empty seat next to Avery. She leaned close, her light floral perfume wrapping around me, pushing away the unwelcome scent of hot dogs and popcorn. I wasn't a wimp, but I also was not a sadist. And going to the hockey game was asking for Luke's attention, and therefore, trouble.

My chin rose, and my resolve hardened. I was being ridiculous. He could bring it. There wasn't anything he could do that would break me.

Avery chatted with her friends for a few minutes, but when she snorted, I pocketed my phone that I was scrolling through and followed her gaze to where Chase stood in front of the bench, arms crossed, gaze scanning the seats around us like he was waiting for trouble. Even at the top as the guys were, they had enemies, especially on the other school's team. That was probably what was setting her brother and Jax even more on edge.

Jax watched. It was subtle, barely noticeable. But I saw it. The way his jaw ticked. After checking the crowd seated around us, his gaze kept returning to Avery. For someone who wasn't supposed to care, Jax sure seemed interested in Chase's sister.

The coach pulled the team's attention to him. A hush swept through the crowd right before announcements, and the national anthem was sung. Then the game started, and a thrill raced through my body. The first line took to the ice, and when I watched Luke skate into position, something in my chest tightened. I couldn't look away as the puck dropped, and our team went on the offensive.

He was in his element. Unstoppable. The star of Blackwood, slicing through the rink as if it was his. I recognized how he called the play with a nod, the way the others—Jax, Chase, even Theo—adjusted without hesitation. Jax delivered a check that sent a guy sprawling. Chase set up a screen just long enough for Theo to rocket the puck into the net. And Luke? He controlled the rhythm. The energy. The outcome. The same way he used to control every heartbeat in my chest.

He skated like he was born for this—sharp, powerful, precise. The crowd chanted his name after a breakaway goal that left the other team stunned.

And me? I just sat there, trying not to remember what it felt like to be the one he looked for in the stands. Now, he didn't even have to look at me to make it clear where we stood.

The game ended in victory—of course it did. Blackwood didn't lose. Not with Luke leading them.

I was up and moving before anyone else in our row. A quick goodbye to Avery and I hurried into the aisle and pushed my way up the stairs and toward the closest exit.

The crowd spilled out, buzzing with energy and school pride. People pushed past, shouting, laughing, wrapped in the post-win high. Avery, not far behind, disappeared into the press of bodies, probably off to keep her overprotective brother from getting into it with someone from Crestview.

By the time I got to my car, my stomach twisted at the sight. A gaping hole was in my driver's side tire where someone had carved a slice in it. I ticked through my options, discarding all two of them—call my mom or roadside assistance. Making this more of an issue would be what whoever had done this wanted.

Not wanting an audience, I climbed into the driver's seat and marked time. When most of the cars around me had pulled out, the parking lot almost empty, I got out. Bending down, I popped the trunk and then went to the back to pull out the jack and my spare tire. I wasn't helpless. I positioned the jack into place and got to work.

I thought I was in the clear, but I didn't get far with changing the tire before I felt him. Luke stepped beside me.

I pushed up to my feet and stood before him, allowing defiance to paint across my expression.

His presence was suffocating. His gaze, lethal. "Seems you have an admirer."

"Not the kind I want." The comment was dual sided, the hit making its presence known as his gaze shuttered even more.

He took the lug wrench from me and quickly changed to the spare, depositing the slashed tire in the trunk. I lowered the jack and tossed the tools in too before closing the trunk. It didn't mean anything, what he'd done. And he made sure to let me know with the icy stare sent my way.

"I know what your mom did," he snapped. "And now you're back like nothing happened?"

"You don't know a damn thing," I fired back, but inside, I froze for half a second at the possibility that he knew more than I thought he did. Or that he was somehow involved. But he couldn't be. He was bluffing. That tick in his jaw. I was sure of it. He couldn't know that we'd burned through some of the money just to survive. I sure as hell wasn't going to admit to what my mom had taken, whether it was directly from his dad's company or the VP boyfriend, like Mom had said.

That damn muscle in his jaw jumped, and panic laced my blood. Even worse—he probably thought he knew everything.

"You disappeared," his voice was icy. "After a chunk of money vanished from the books, your mom bailed and took you with her. And somehow, my dad was left holding the fallout."

I sucked in a breath. *He doesn't know the truth.* Not all of it. But if he kept digging—if he found out what really happened… everything could unravel, and we would be in even more danger. All he thought he knew was that my mom stole money from his dad's company and that I'd used him. That last part wasn't true. I hadn't cared about his financial worth then, and I didn't now.

His eyes narrowed, seeming to clue in that I was hiding something from him. "You think I won't find out? I will."

I angled my chin higher. "Then I guess we'll both be surprised." I waved to the tire as I opened my door. "Thanks for that, even though I know it didn't mean anything." The car started with the push of a button, and I drove off, leaving him standing there. I paused at the stop sign before the main road and glanced back.

Luke was still there, standing exactly where I'd left him, chest rising as though he'd sprinted a mile.

For one second, I saw him—not the arrogant hockey god but the guy who used to trace stars on my skin when no one was watching. And it hurt more than it should've.

I shut the door on the thought—and him.

CHAPTER EIGHT

LUKE

Several days passed. Mila and Avery got close again—too close for Chase's liking. He didn't say it, but it showed. The fists curling when they laughed in the hallway. The way his eyes tracked Mila when she wasn't looking, sharp with dread.

It wasn't about jealousy. Not that kind of thing. Chase just didn't want Avery dragged into something she couldn't climb out of. He didn't trust Mila not to disappear again. Not to hurt his sister.

And I got it. Because I didn't trust her either. But it wasn't that simple.

None of us said it out loud, but we all felt it—pieces shifting on a chessboard we couldn't fully see. Someone else was moving them, and sooner or later, we would be forced to play.

I hated it. Because the minute I moved onto that board, I stepped into my father's world. The one built on silence, shadows, and power plays. The one where he'd ordered me to stay the hell away from Mila. The one I'd been trying to outrun since I was old enough to realize what the King name actually meant.

When Dad or Lorne wanted something, people got hurt. I

wasn't a good guy, far from it. But what they did? That was something I'd dreaded stepping into.

But maybe I was already in it. Maybe I always had been. The slip of paper with Lorne's signature okaying the sale of the boardwalk building seemed like a segue in, as well as Drew's hint that Dad was stressed and they needed me there sooner rather than later.

Mila being back only made it worse. She was in classes with at least one of us. Easy to keep tabs on and watch. And I did. Constantly.

At first it was surveillance. Resentment. Every time I saw her, I thought about what we had been—what we could've been—and how she'd ripped that away without explanation. But the longer she stayed, the more it twisted into something else. She wasn't flinching under Elise's games. She wasn't playing the victim. And damn if it didn't piss me off that she still had that fire.

The kind that burned slow, dangerous, and permanent. She hadn't broken. And that, somehow, made me want to push her even more.

In last class, her hair slid over one shoulder, leaving her neck bare. No silver chain. No charm. Just skin where the necklace used to rest, right against her collarbone. My jaw locked. It didn't matter how much I told myself I didn't give a damn—it still felt like a punch. A gap that didn't just mark what was missing—it reminded me who'd taken it away.

After last period, I barely made it to my locker before Elise appeared. She leaned against the metal, all cool composure and silent threat, clearly waiting. Her perfume clung to the air—sweet, heady, and all wrong.

"You know," she purred, voice silky, "I could've helped you."

I didn't even glance at her, just played the game like Dad wanted. "With what?"

Her smile sharpened, all teeth—as if she'd already marked the kill. "The version of the story people hear about her." She stepped closer, her hip brushing mine, intentional. "You and me —we worked. We could again. Make it official, and maybe I'll forget the Mila crap never happened."

I stared at her, hollow. "We were never together. You were a warm body. That was it."

Elise's smirk didn't falter. She was too trained for that. "Maybe. But that's not what people remember. And I can remind them, if you want her gone. Just stop pretending you don't care about that. Or someone else will handle it. And it won't be pretty."

There it was. The veiled threat. The test. She wanted to see if I still cared. If she could twist it into leverage. Elise never made a move unless she could collect later. She was clueless in one thing—I was never interested in her, and that wasn't going to change with Mila here or not.

I stepped in close, voice low. "You need to back off. You don't know what you're stepping into."

Her fingers danced along the locker handles, nails clicking, a timer counting down. "Suit yourself. But if she keeps overstepping her worth, she won't last long here." She looked back once, eyes shining like broken glass. "You'll come around. You always do. And when you do, I'll still be here."

She walked off like she hadn't just started a fire. I stood there, teeth grinding, until the bell shrieked above and the crowd thinned.

Practice didn't help. I hit the ice, pushed harder than usual. But I still couldn't skate off the bitterness she'd left behind. By the time we got to the locker room, I was raw. My gear peeled off like a second skin, sweat soaking into the rubber floors.

Chase muttered to himself as he shoved stuff into his bag. "Gotta keep an eye on Avery next game. She keeps talking to these guys like—"

Jax's head snapped up. "Who?"

We always wondered which guy had wrecked Avery enough to make her shrink like she had. That was why we watched so closely. Why Chase lost his mind about anyone circling his sister.

The tension crackled, a snapped cable. Chase turned slowly. "You got something to say?"

Theo stilled, his dirty blond hair slicked back from sweat, eyes bouncing between them.

Jax rolled his shoulders, casually, but his voice was clipped. "Just wondering if it was someone from Crestview. Something we need to handle." His jaw was a steel trap.

The two locked eyes, and for a second, I thought Jax might throw down right there. But Chase muttered something under his breath and looked away. Interesting.

We finished packing in silence. Once outside, we decided to grab food. Nothing major—just a place with decent burgers not far from the arena. As we rolled into the parking lot, Avery's car was already there, parked under a flickering sign. Through the window, I spotted her in a booth. Mila was there too—along with two other girls Avery usually hung out with.

They were laughing. Mila's head tilted back, her gray-green eyes bright. For a second, something in my chest tugged sideways.

Chase saw it too. He exhaled, tension rolling off his shoulders. "At least Avery's smiling again. Before everything implodes."

I didn't say anything. They knew about what Elise had said. We were waiting, watching. Even with all that, my gut clenched at the sight of Mila. I remembered that smile. I remembered how it used to be for me.

And maybe—stupid as it was—part of me wanted to deserve that smile again. But this world didn't allow fragile things. Not with Elise scheming. Not with Dad watching. Not with danger closing in on the people I couldn't stop thinking about.

I stepped out of the car, hands in my pockets, and watched Mila from across the lot. She didn't see me. But I saw her. And I wasn't sure if I was guarding her from the world. Or from myself.

CHAPTER NINE

MILA

The next day, I was halfway to my next class, digging through my bag for my phone, when I heard the determined clack of heels across polished floors. I didn't even need to look to know Elise was closing in.

"Mila." Elise's voice was sugar-drenched steel. "Got a second?"

She didn't announce herself. She never needed to. She appeared, Nina and Tori trailing a step behind, their eyes darting as if uncertain whether they were backup or witnesses.

I didn't answer. Just pivoted, keeping my face blank.

"You've been busy." She smiled, as if I'd already lost. "Attempting to reclaim old territory. Flirting with someone who isn't yours."

She stepped closer, eyes wide that went flat with steel. "Let's skip the fake smiles and get to the part where you leave. Again."

My hand curled into a fist.

Elise checked her manicure. "Because if you don't disappear soon, someone's going to make sure you do. And next time, it won't be gentle, or by your choice."

The hallway thinned as the bell rang. Seconds—maybe less—

before the crowd vanished completely. As students ducked into classrooms, my sightline to Theo and Jax cleared. Both watching. Hawk-eyed and silent.

Tori, Elise's ever-loyal shadow, looked like she wanted to melt into the floor.

Behind her, Theo leaned against the wall, thumbs tapping at his phone. Disinterested—or pretending to be. But I knew better. He was watching. They both were.

I couldn't tell if they'd heard what Elise said or if they already knew. Either way, slow, simmering heat sparked low in my gut. If they were in on this, if they were helping her twist the knife, we'd have words. Real ones.

But neither of them moved. And I bet they wouldn't, not until someone else made the first play. I wouldn't give them the satisfaction.

Elise leaned in, her cloying perfume choking me with its proximity. "Luke's already mine. So is this school. You? You don't even register."

I met her gaze, steady. "You sure sound threatened for someone who claims to rule everything."

Her smile twitched. "I'm not threatened. I'm just done playing nice."

Then she turned, hair flipping over her shoulder, heels striking the floor like punctuation marks as she walked away.

Tori—Theo's not-quite girlfriend—bit her lip, avoiding my eyes. Nina, Elise's other loyal minion and social ladder-climber, seemed to be loving every second of the scene. She followed, but Tori hesitated. Just for a second. And then she was gone too.

Seconds after, the guys left too, heading to the cafeteria, Leaving me in the hallway, back pressed to the locker, already planning the next move. This wasn't just about jealousy. This was about erasure. A declaration of war with a body count. Because that threat? It carried bodily harm.

I rolled my shoulders back, pivoted, and stalked toward the

cafeteria. My fight wasn't really with Elise; it was with Luke—always with him. The second I smacked my palms on the hockey team's lunch table, the room went still. Conversations cut off mid-word. Luke sat dead center, elbows braced on the table, fingers drumming out a slow, controlled rhythm. His kingdom. His court. His silence.

He looked up—calm, indifferent. Cold.

"What kind of king lets his lackeys deliver his messages?" I said loud enough for the whole room to hear.

Chase snorted into his soda. Theo's mouth twitched. Jax raised a brow like I'd just offered to arm wrestle death. Luke didn't blink.

"You let your little followers issue threats?" I snapped. "You think that makes you powerful?"

His eyes narrowed. Tap-tap-tap—his fingers stopped.

And then he stood. I expected words. Retaliation. Something sharp and strategic. What I got was his hand—warm and hard—closing around my wrist. Heat shot up my arm. Not painful. Not forceful. Just… undeniable.

He dragged me out of the cafeteria. Every eye followed. Elise's smirk faltered when she saw his hand on me. Her world didn't account for deviations in the script.

The hallway was silent. Lockers stretched out on either side like lined-up soldiers in a standoff. Luke pushed me gently against the wall, his hand slamming beside my head, body caging mine without touching. He wasn't angry. He was seething.

"You don't know what you've started." His voice crawled over my skin, making it hum.

"Then enlighten me."

"You keep poking shit you don't understand—my family, Elise, the people who don't care how many bodies they bury to stay clean."

"Oh, so I should be scared of your friends?"

"No." He stepped in, chest brushing mine. "You should be scared of what happens when I'm not there to stop them."

"Interesting," I murmured. "You think you're the hero in this story even when you don't lift a finger to do anything different than orchestrate the carnage?"

"I think you don't know how close you are to getting hurt."

"Funny." My gaze locked on his. "I could say the same about you."

His breath was warm against my cheek, and for one insane second, I thought he would kiss me. Thought he would bridge the chasm he'd built with silence and rage and distance. The one I'd initially carved between us. But he didn't.

Instead, his fingers lifted—slow, reverent—and brushed the curve of my jaw. My breath caught. His eyes darkened.

And just that fast, the world snapped out of the present and jarred me backward into the past. It was late. The rink had emptied hours ago, save for the low thrum of the compressor and the distant tap of my broom against the concrete.

I'd been wiping down the benches when he skated over, breathless and flushed, hair plastered to his forehead beneath his helmet.

"Don't leave yet," he said, tugging his gloves off with his teeth. "Skate with me."

"I'm not exactly dressed for it," I said, glancing down at my hoodie and jeans. "No Skates. I'll trip."

He grinned, that slow, crooked one that always knocked the air out of me. "I'll hold you up."

Then he pulled a pair of skates from behind his back—my size, of course. He always noticed the details no one else did.

That night, he didn't let go of my hand. Not once. We circled the rink in silence, the scrape of his blades carving a rhythm into the ice. My fingers were frozen. My cheeks flushed. But his hand—his grip—was warm, grounding. Like he could keep me upright just by willing it.

After a while, he pulled me gently toward the penalty box, climbed in first before reaching for me again, like letting go even for a second wasn't an option.

I sat beside him, breath clouding in the air between us, and he just stared forward like he was watching something only he could see.

Then, softer than I'd ever heard him, "I can't do it."

My chest tightened. "Do what?"

"King Enterprises. The board meetings. The handshakes. The empire." His voice thinned, brittle at the edges. "It's a cage they've spent my whole life building."

"But you're good at it," I said. Because he was. He could command a room with half a smirk and a perfectly measured pause. He knew how to talk numbers like they were a second language. He wore legacy like a fitted suit.

"Being good at something doesn't mean it feeds you." His thumb brushed mine again, slow and searching. "But on the ice…"

He finally turned toward me then. And whatever he saw in my face cracked something in his.

"…on the ice, I breathe."

His words lodged in my ribs. But it was the look in his eyes that made my heart forget how to beat—hollowed out and hungry, like he was drowning in a world that kept shoving his head underwater. And still, somehow, he looked at me like I was air.

His voice dropped. "I think about you. All the damn time."

The confession hit like a slap and a balm at once.

"I try not to," he said. "Try to focus, train, pretend this"—his thumb pressed against my knuckles—"wasn't the best part of my day. But it always is. It always was."

I couldn't breathe.

"I want you in a way that doesn't shut off. It's not just the way you look, though yeah, you walk into a room, and I'm done for. It's how you see things. How you don't bullshit me. You make it hard to lie to myself. Even when I want to."

His fingers tightened around mine. "If it ever comes down to a choice between legacy and oxygen…" He leaned in then, forehead brushing mine. His voice was a whisper meant only for me. "I'll choose the ice. I'll choose breathing." Another beat. "I'll choose you."

And I knew he meant it. In that moment, under the arena lights, I felt it like gravity. He would burn the whole kingdom down if it meant keeping me. And maybe that was why I kissed him. Soft, slow, reverent. As if I was telling him—*I see you, I want you; I'm scared as hell, but I'm still here.*

His mouth moved against mine, starved and certain. And for a while, we forgot the world waiting outside the rink. Forgot our names, our duties, the minefields we would eventually have to cross.

In that box, we weren't heirs or outcasts. We were just a boy who wanted to breathe and a girl who wanted to be enough. And for one night—we were.

But that was before.

His past touch vanished, and I jolted back into the present.

He eased back. Didn't speak. Everything in me ached with the echo of that night—the truth he'd shared, the promise he'd never kept because I'd left.

"We'll see who breaks first," he whispered.

I smirked, lifting my chin. "Spoiler alert—it won't be me."

He dropped his hand as if I'd burned him and stepped away. Didn't say another word. Didn't look back. But his jaw was tight. His fists clenched. And every part of his walk away screamed one thing—this wasn't over. Not even close.

Later, when I went to my next class, I passed Logan near the science wing. He was whispering to Elise—too close, too hushed.

The words carried: *"Take care of it."*

Logan's dark eyes caught mine, his smile all teeth and no warmth. Elise didn't turn around.

Unease crawled down my spine for the first time since I got back. I held his stare, pretending not to flinch. But deep down, I knew—I'd miscalculated. Badly.

CHAPTER TEN

LUKE

In my locker was a piece of paper folded with surgical precision. There was one line in black ink: *She shouldn't be here. Fix it.*

My jaw clenched so hard it felt like bone cracking. The handwritten note felt heavier than paper. Loaded.

I didn't need to guess who sent it. Elise had been circling me for days—smirking, provoking, waiting for me to finally snap and drive Mila out of Blackwood for good.

But Elise didn't give orders. Not to me. I crumpled the paper, shoved it into my pocket, and headed down the hall.

I found her exactly where I expected—leaning back against the lockers near the senior wing, French-manicured finger scrolling her phone.

"Elise."

She looked up, smirk ready. "Luke. To what do I owe the pleasure?"

I extracted the note and held it between two fingers.

Still nothing in her eyes. She scanned the paper, voice casual: "A reminder. You've been… distracted."

My response was quiet, cold. "You think I need help handling Mila?"

She shrugged, stepping closer until her perfume was choking me. "You seem to." She paused, smile slipping just enough to expose a flash of greed. "You've got too much on your plate. Your father. The whispers. The company. Let a little scandal hit, and everything folds."

I blinked. "What are you talking about?"

Her tone stayed syrupy. "You forget—my dad has a front-row seat to the cleanup crew. Dunn Industries might not wear the same crest as King Enterprises, but they're in the same bed when it matters."

She leaned in, voice dropping to a purr. "Mila's mom already made waves once. Disappearing only bought her time. If she starts poking around again… someone might decide she's a risk to overlook."

Cold crawled down my spine. "Elise," I growled. "Pull it back. You're digging your own grave." I took a breath—and dropped the bomb. "Family business isn't part of this. And you? You were a mistake—just someone I used once or twice, nothing more." The play nice mandate from my father didn't apply here. I drew the line at encouraging a relationship between us. There never had been one, nor would it ever happen.

Her eyes darkened. Rage showed for a heartbeat, then she swallowed it. Instead, she dragged a fingertip down my chest. "People remember what I tell them. A twist here, a lie there—and suddenly, we're history again."

I grabbed her wrist before she could pull back. My grip was steel, controlled. "Don't drag me into your games. Or you'll regret it."

Recognition flickered in her eyes. Not fear—but respect. She slid back, saying, "Fine. But… if I didn't write the note?"

I leveled my stare. "Then we've got a bigger problem." Even

as I said it, I knew she was lying. Or someone else was pulling her strings. Either way, she was the one that dropped the threat into my locker because I recognized her handwriting.

Later, I found myself outside, leaning against the iron railing near the athletic quad after school and before practice. Mila walked across campus, bag slung over one shoulder, the wind tugging at her dark hair. She paused, brushing it away with a flick of defiance.

Her fingers brushed the hollow of her throat, as if reaching for something long gone. For a second, I almost asked her why. Then I remembered—I already knew. I'd been holding the reason in my hand the night she walked away.

She didn't know I watched. And this time, I wasn't tracking her to figure out how to break her. I was keeping tabs because she might be in deeper trouble than even she knew.

Between Elise's threats, the note, Dad's warning, and what I overheard last week—mentions of money, damage control, someone cleaning up—I saw a pattern. I knew too much to ignore it.

I went inside and took it to the ice, hoping the cold would carve the noise from my head. But after two hours of drills and contact, the only thing I managed to shake was the skin off my knuckles. The storm stayed.

Later, I headed home, mind scrolling through scenarios. I walked through the front door aimlessly until I found myself in the kitchen. I paused, the dark feeling heavier here. Barefoot, water glass in hand, I stared through the window at empty streets.

I didn't hear Drew until he was already moving in— sparkling water in his hand, face calm.

"Couldn't sleep either?" he asked.

I shook my head. "Just thinking."

He twisted the cap off the water and leaned against the counter. "Thinking's a dangerous game at 2 a.m."

I thought again of the note. "You ever wonder if we don't know everything about Dad... about the company?"

He took a slow sip, eyes steady. "Dad built this from nothing. That kind of power always leaves blood behind." He set the chilled bottle down.

"You sound like him."

He shrugged. "I used to hate it. Now I get it."

I put my hands on the counter. "And you think he's hiding something?"

He offered a faint, unreadable smile. "He's always ten steps ahead. If there's something he's hiding, it's not bullshit. It's why you shouldn't worry."

My eyes flicked to the hallway that led to his home office. "What if it's already in motion?"

His tone softened. "Then you deal with it. But don't forget who you are—and where you came from." He shoved off the counter and strolled away. "Try to sleep, bro. You've got a game tomorrow. And, Luke?"—he waited until I met his eyes—"I'll handle the company. Nothing's falling on your shoulders. School. College. That's your job."

My brother was trying to protect me, which I appreciated. Part of me recognized that he'd come into his own, that he thrived in dad's world, that it had become his. And maybe he would even shoulder that weight for me too, but that wasn't really me. I didn't let anyone take on my battles, and this one felt like it was headed my way.

I stayed long after he left, the note heavy in my pocket. One way or another, I had to decide what Mila meant to me—liability, or something I couldn't let go.

CHAPTER ELEVEN

MILA

The rink was silent. Just the faint hum of overhead lights. The soft scrape of my blades against the ice. My breath, jagged and shallow, echoed back—not even mine anymore. Here, the noise in my head dulled.

This was the one place that still gave me a thrill, probably because it used to be ours—mine and Luke's. When things were simple. Not the borrowed bedrooms or rundown rentals. Not the fake smiles and quick getaways. Just this—cold, clean, endless. The sound of nothing and the feel of flight. The rink was peace before I knew what peace cost. Before we knew what was coming. Before he became the guy who looked at me with anger and hate. Before it all fractured.

I pushed harder, faster, slicing across the smooth surface until my thighs burned and my lungs ached—as if speed alone could strip the truth from my ribs. But I didn't get far.

"What the hell do you think you're doing here?" His voice cut through the quiet, sharp as a slap.

I skidded to a stop, the scrape of my blades loud in the stillness. My pulse spiked, breath catching as I turned. Luke stood just off the ice, arms folded, his posture tight. Like he was holding something back. Or barely holding on.

"Clearing my head," I said, flatly. I didn't mention the key I'd kept from working here sophomore year. "Didn't realize I needed a permission slip."

His smirk was all ice. "Everything here belongs to me."

I scoffed. "Sure. The rink. The school. The whole damn town. Your kingdom, right?"

He stepped onto the ice without hesitation, like the cold bent around him. Each stride was smooth. Controlled. Dangerous.

"No," he said, low and lethal. "Just you."

My heart stuttered. But I didn't flinch. "You're delusional." *I used to be his.*

He kept coming. Calm. Calculated. "And you're reckless. Breaking in here in the middle of the night?"

"Maybe I needed to get away from your bullshit."

Something shifted in his eyes. Not anger. Something worse. "You think it's that easy to escape it?"

"What's that supposed to mean?" My voice was thin. Tight.

Luke ran a hand through his hair, exhaling hard. For a second, he looked like the guy who made me laugh on this very ice. The one who let me forget the world for a minute. Then the wall snapped back into place.

"Your mom's a thief," he said flatly. "It's gonna catch up with her."

The air left my lungs. "What?" I barely recognized my own voice.

He moved closer. I didn't back away.

"You heard me."

"That's not true." My head shook before the words even formed. "You don't know what you're talking about."

His jaw clenched. "I know exactly what I'm talking about. My dad told me. The embezzlement. Your mom. Darren

Langley—the VP she was dating. He vanished right after the money did. Then your mom ran. Do the math."

Suffocating cold spread through my chest. "You think she had something to do with that?" My voice cracked. "With his disappearance?"

"I think she saw an opportunity—and took it."

"No," I whispered, but it didn't sound like a denial. Not anymore. Because I remembered. Her panicked whisper—*We can't stay. We saw too much.* The metallic tang of blood thick in the air. The duffel bag, stuffed with cash. Her hands shaking so badly she could barely zip it. I never asked who killed him; I never pushed if she was more involved.

Luke's gaze never left me. "You didn't know."

I shook my head, slower this time. All he referenced was the money. And yeah, I knew about it, but that it came from Darren —that was what I knew. His death? That wasn't public knowledge. The certainty over where the cash came from drained out of me like the warmth in my fingers. He skated even closer, his presence a wall I didn't know how to get around.

"You think you're safe here?" His voice was all edge, lethal. "You have no idea who you're playing with."

My temper snapped back into place like a shield. "Then tell me."

He blinked.

"What happened between our families?" I asked, stepping toward him. "Why do you hate us so much? What aren't you saying?"

Because this—this fear curling in my stomach—it wasn't new. Mom had been hiding things my whole life. Codes and cover stories. Whispers behind closed doors. Things she used to share with me—and me only. But lately, there was too much silence. I'd always thought she was the smartest person in the room. Now I wasn't sure I even knew who she was.

Luke's face closed off so fast it almost hurt. Whatever truth had flickered there vanished.

"Go home, Mila."

"No. Not until you—"

"Now."

His voice cracked like a whip.

Then he was gone—pushing past me, disappearing into the shadows at the far end of the rink. I stood there, skates locked in place, body trembling from more than the cold.

We can't stay. We saw too much. Her voice curled through my mind like a vice, choking me. What the hell had really happened? And why did it feel like everything—everything between Luke and me—was about to explode?

The worst part wasn't that he got to me. It was that some traitorous part of me still wanted to believe he meant it—that buried under all the anger, the guy who once chose me over everything wasn't gone.

And that maybe, deep down, I hadn't either. Because when he looked at me—really looked—I felt myself becoming the version I used to trust. The one who believed in art. In love. In something more than damage control.

CHAPTER TWELVE

LUKE

Elbows flew. Sneakers squeaked. Sweat hung heavy. Gym class was a pressure cooker. No coach in sight, just testosterone, grudges, and too much to prove. I clocked Elise and Logan whispering as they slipped in late, their body language tight. Elise threw a look over her shoulder—first at Mila then at me.

Logan's dad was out of King Enterprises. Bitter. Sniffing around Dunn Industries. That kind of fall never went unanswered.

We were playing basketball in gym class. But it felt like a battlefield.

Mila had the ball. She moved as if she didn't give a damn about who was watching—but she had to know Logan was. His eyes tracked her the way a predator watches prey.

She crossed left then blew past him as though he wasn't there. Except he was. His smirk widened. I saw it before it happened—too far away to stop it but close enough to feel the hit in my gut.

He stepped into her path and clipped her ankle. Her body folded. One second flying, the next—her knee cracked against the floor. Louder than the whistle that never came. A curse slipped from her lips as she crumpled.

Everything inside me snapped. The decision I'd been weighing about Mila was made, solidified in one move too far against her. I pushed through bodies. Grabbed Logan by the shirt and slammed him back. His head bounced off the cinderblock, echoing through the gym.

"What the fuck was that?"

His smirk faltered. "Relax, King. It was an accident."

Bullshit. My knuckles itched. Theo and Jax hovered at the edge of the court. Watching. Waiting. My team. But not just mine. Mila's too, once I made it known I would protect her. That was clear—if they didn't move, didn't interfere, that meant something. A shift in loyalty.

Before I could decide what to do with him, Mila was on her feet. Wobbly, but standing. Her eyes locked on mine. Searching. As if she wasn't sure what version of me she was looking at.

She didn't say a word. Just brushed off her hands and limped off the court like it didn't hurt. Like she hadn't just been taken down. And it killed me that she didn't look back.

After practice, the locker room stank of body spray, sweat, and post-game bravado. Most of the guys had cleared out, except for a few still jostling around the benches.

Jax shoved a towel into his gym locker. "You good?" His tone was careful.

"Why wouldn't I be?"

Theo grunted, leaning against the locker beside mine. "Logan's an idiot. He's lashing out, and not only here. On the ice. If Coach doesn't handle it, someone should."

I didn't answer. Didn't need to.

Jax exchanged a glance with Theo then clapped my shoulder once before heading out.

"We've got your back. Just figure out what she is to you," Theo muttered before following.

The room echoed with the sound of the door shutting after they left. Empty but not quiet. When I followed out the same exit of the locker room, Mila was waiting, just past the weight racks. She stepped into my path as if she belonged there. Like she was daring me to go around her.

"What's your deal?" Her voice was low, aggravated. "You screw with my head, let your little fan club take shots, and then the second someone else steps in, you're ready to throw down?"

"It's not that simple." But the gnawing in my gut—stronger whenever she was near—said otherwise.

She scoffed, folding her arms. "Seems like it is. You didn't use to let anyone else fight your battles. Isn't that what this is?"

I shook my head, not willing to explain or go deep into what was changing, or what I had allowed to happen on Elise's behalf before today. I crossed my arms. "No one lays a hand on you. Not like that."

"Right. Because only *you* get to do damage."

My jaw clenched.

"Tell me, Luke,"—her voice dropped to a whisper—"if you hate me so much… why do you care?"

Silence stretched between us. Then I stepped close enough to feel the heat of her skin. To smell the citrus and salt of her sweat.

She didn't move. But her breath hitched. Mine did the same. "Because I hate that I can't hate you."

Her lips parted. That fire in her eyes flickered—uncertain. For a second, I nearly reached for her. My hand twitched at my side. A breath from brushing against her skin.

But I didn't. I backed up. Turned and walked off before I did something I couldn't undo. Before I begged her to let me stay. Before I gave in to the one thing I couldn't afford to want.

CHAPTER THIRTEEN

MILA

Luke's gaze clung to me after gym class when I'd confronted him. I felt the heat of it long after I walked away. A phantom touch buzzing under my skin, low and steady. He'd stepped in. Luke-fucking-King. I was used to his hate. Expected it.

He was the last person I needed saving me. The last one I wanted tangled in my mess. But he did it anyway. Now I had no idea what to do with that.

The hallway swallowed me whole, the stares cutting in a little deeper today. More deliberate. I clocked the micro-reactions—the slow blink of a girl's mascara-clumped lashes as I passed, the shift of a guy's stance as if he was bracing for a hit that never came. Someone angled their phone just high enough to snap a pic before pretending to scroll.

My pulse beat a little harder. They were figuring out which side to be on—Luke's or Elise's. It shouldn't be a contest. When —*if*—he made his stance crystal clear with me, it wouldn't be.

Avery slid in beside me as if she'd been shadowing my route for blocks. She didn't say hi. Just murmured, "Don't shoot the messenger—but Elise is saying your mom got you into Blackwood using sex. And she dragged your name into it too."

I didn't flinch. Not on the outside. Inside, a white-hot flare of rage shot through my chest. "Seriously?"

She gave a humorless smile. "You know her strategy. Whisper it loud enough, long enough... it sticks." Her jaw locked. Tension roped down her neck. "She's ramping up. Hoping you'll snap and give her an audience."

I let out a bitter laugh. "Creative. I'll give her that."

Avery didn't laugh. Her gaze darted across the hallway like she was tracking threats. We detoured near the vending machines, half-shielded from view. It wasn't private, but it would do.

"She's also bringing your mom into it." Her voice lowered. "Said she has a reputation."

The words strangled the air in my lungs. "Of course she did." Because of course Elise would drag my mother into this. It wasn't enough to gut me. She wanted a full dissection. Like mother, like daughter—that was the line she would push. And it wasn't completely off base, was it? How else were we able to afford Blackwood Academy's tuition fee?

Mom had always gone after powerful men. Charismatic. Dangerous, sometimes. She played the game better than anyone. Bent truth the way light bends through a prism. And if the rumors were true—if she was sleeping with the principal—then this wasn't just smoke. It was fire. One I would need to put out before it torched everything.

A conversation with my mom sprang to mind—I'd asked her how we could afford the Academy, especially as we'd blown through our savings. Her response was *I've got it handled.* And now I knew how.

A heavy silence bloomed between us. Avery didn't fill it. Just stared at the gum stuck to the base of the vending machine as if it had answers.

Finally, she sighed. "The guys are closing rank."

I frowned. "What does that mean?" I wasn't in their circle. I no longer mattered.

"It means you've been brought back in. Word's spreading about what went down in gym class. They're backing you. You've got their protection, at least to a degree. Not sure how that'll go with Elise, though."

That wasn't all she had to say. Something else was eating at her. I leaned back against the wall, arms folded. "And?"

"And Chase…" Her voice dipped, as though saying it too loud might make it worse. "He's watching me. More than usual."

I straightened, catching the hint she was throwing. That maybe she wanted my help with her brother, or at the very least, my ear. But I also had noticed why Chase was more on edge, even if she wasn't ready to admit it. "Because of Jax?"

Avery's lashes flicked up in surprise. Then down again. She worried the sleeve of her T-shirt between her fingers.

"He's not exactly subtle," I added. "I see the way he hovers when your brother isn't looking. The way his jaw tightens when someone else gets too close."

She flinched—barely—but it was there. "Jax doesn't care about me like that."

The words came out flat. Practiced. I didn't challenge her. But I didn't believe her either. She believed it—clearly—but Jax? That guy watched her as if she was both a complication and a lifeline—touching her might break something in him, but staying away was killing him anyway. He just hadn't figured out which yet, or if he could go against his best friend's wishes and pursue her without causing an all-out war.

"You know that's not true, right?" I said quietly. "You're one of the few people Jax actually listens to. He would throw down against anyone for you, Aves. And we both know that's not nothing for a guy like him."

"Yeah. Maybe." Her smile didn't reach her eyes. "He might throw a punch—but that doesn't mean he'll choose me."

I pushed off the wall and leaned against the vending machines with her. "Then make him."

That pulled her attention. She blinked. "What?"

"Make him choose you." I shrugged. "Be brave, Aves. You're one of the smartest people here." The girl was in contention to be valedictorian. She didn't really want it, but she could. "You want him? Don't wait for permission, especially from your brother. He's never gonna give it."

Avery opened her mouth. Closed it. And then she smiled. For real this time. "Who are you, and what have you done with Mila?"

I smirked. "Don't get used to it."

Her laugh was soft. Then she checked her phone and cursed under her breath. "Shit. I'm late for physics."

I nudged her shoulder with mine. "Go. I'll catch up."

She jogged off without another word. I stayed. Just long enough to let the cold from the vending machine seep into my back. Long enough to feel the tension fizzing out, only to be replaced by something worse.

The day crawled by. And the entire time? I could still feel Luke's stare from earlier—the one that haunted my spine. And I had a sinking feeling he wasn't done with me yet. The rules of the game had just changed.

I took that thought with me throughout the rest of the day and until I was at home where I could finally do something without anyone hovering over me.

By the time I got home, the sky had bled into night. My fingers hovered over my laptop's keyboard, the blue light of the screen the only thing illuminating my room. The ceiling fan creaked above me. A faint hum of traffic drifted through the barely cracked window. The scent of cheap detergent and lemon floor cleaner clung to the air—remnants from my half-hearted cleaning job on the dump we were living in. I'd been here for three hours, maybe more. Time didn't exist in this kind of obsession.

Click. Scroll. Click again.

Archived press releases. Blog posts no one read. It was all there. Buried under layers of PR polish and corporate vagueness. I searched local business forums, legal filings, finance blogs desperate for ad revenue—anywhere that might've caught something the mainstream media didn't care enough to report.

And then I found it. A photo from the day Mom and I left Blackwood.

Buried in a puff piece from just over a year ago. The headline was bullshit. Something like *"King Enterprises Ushers in New Era of Leadership."* The article read as a love letter to a dynasty trying not to look desperate in public. Words like "streamlining" and "strategic transition." They meant nothing.

But the image—it gutted me.

A group of executives lined up in front of the building's newly unveiled plaque. Plastic smiles. Suits that cost more than my entire wardrobe. And in the back, slightly off-center but unmistakable, stood my mother.

Wearing a navy blazer. Her mouth in a hard line. Arms folded. Not casual. Not proud. Defensive. And there beside her was Darren Langley. And—the reveal stopped me cold—Lorne. Behind them. The cleanup partner whose face was always out of view. In the last photo before Langley was killed.

My breath caught. She knew Lorne. She was with him the day it all went off the rails. She wasn't just there—she was at the epicenter.

Darren, the boyfriend. The vice president. The one who, according to town legend from what I'd just read, took a high-paying job out of state and ghosted everyone. Only... that was never the story I got. Because I remembered that night. Not a goodbye. Not a moving van.

Blood. A pool of it spreading beneath his body. Copper thick in the air. The panic when she wrapped her arms around me. Whispered, "They'll blame us," as if it was a curse. Like she already knew we were running.

I'd assumed it was a jealous wife. A lover's spat gone sideways. My mom never had healthy relationships—never stuck around long enough for the fallout. But this…? This was bigger. Langley didn't relocate. He disappeared.

The laptop snapped shut so hard it echoed through the small room. I grabbed my phone, thumb shaking as I pulled the image up again and stormed out.

Twenty minutes later, after booking it across town, I was standing in the rink's hallway that still buzzed with post-practice noise. Skate guards clanged as a few stragglers from the team exited the ice. Laughter spilled from the locker rooms.

I spotted him instantly—Luke, leaning against a wall, one earbud in, scrolling through his phone as if the world didn't just shift on its axis.

He didn't see me coming. Good. I shoved my phone against his chest, screen up.

His head snapped up. "What the hell?"

"What is this?"

His brow furrowed as he looked down. The image loaded. His hand froze.

"Where did you get this?" he asked, voice low.

"No. Don't do that. Don't act surprised." I stepped in. "That's my mom. Standing next to the guy your dad called a trusted exec. The one who vanished without so much as a fucking farewell party. And behind them? *Lorne.* You know that's not good. Ever." My voice shook. "If he's there, it means something went sideways. *You* know that."

"You're reading into things that aren't there." Luke's expression didn't change. Not much. But something locked behind his eyes. "And that picture? That's not news."

"Oh, so we're just pretending it's fine that your family buried the truth about a man who disappeared? That my mom was there—literally in the picture—during the 'restructuring'?"

His jaw flexed. "Your mother took money that wasn't hers. She disappeared. She left chaos behind."

"You don't know anything about her."

"I know what my father told me."

I scoffed. "And he's a credible source now? Must be nice, playing loyal son while your entire legacy's rotting from the inside." I wanted to scream that Darren Langley was dead, but that was too far. And it was clear he didn't know. I couldn't trust him, not with how at odds we were.

Luke stepped closer, shoulders squared, voice cutting. "She was involved. With Langley. With whatever happened. She knew where the money went."

"She ran because she was scared." My throat tightened. "You think I knew what was happening? All I knew was we had to leave—again. Another town, more burned bridges. I didn't know—" My breath caught. "I left you without saying goodbye because I didn't have a choice."

He stared at me. Silent. Then: "You ran with her."

The words sliced deeper than I expected and made me complicit, as though he believed I'd known all along.

I staggered back a step. "You have no idea what it was like. What the fuck did you expect me to do—stay behind and live in a cardboard box behind the arena? What other option did I have but to follow my mom? I don't have a trust fund at my disposal like some people do."

His gaze flicked away. Just for a second. Then back. But it was enough.

"You think I wanted any of this?" My voice cracked, but I didn't stop. "I've been carrying this weight for a while. And now I find out your family's version of events was never the full story?" I knew I wasn't making sense to him because he didn't have the full story. Neither did I, but I had a hell of a lot more than he did.

He didn't answer. Didn't argue. Just turned and walked away. No apology. No closure. Just… gone.

I stood there, the image still glowing on my phone, heart jackhammering against my ribs. Every part of me vibrating with the awful, gut-deep realization that this wasn't about school rivalries or reputations anymore. And somehow, Elise was wading in just as deep.

This was blood-deep. Legacy-deep. And whatever I found next might not just burn bridges. It might blow up the whole damn town.

CHAPTER FOURTEEN

LUKE

The shift hit the second I stepped inside. The locker room dipped into silence, as if I'd stepped into a conversation I wasn't meant to hear. My presence was something they hadn't prepared for.

Logan, never one to shut the hell up, leaned back on the bench and threw out a smirk that was too damn pleased with itself. "You're getting sloppy, King."

"She's not yours to mess with, asshole. Stay the fuck away from her." The rest I left in my stare. It shut him the hell up, and he bent his head, finished unlacing his skates, and left the locker room.

Chase closed his locker hard enough to make the metal ring. "He's not wrong. One minute you're telling us to steer clear, the next you're playing fucking bodyguard."

My jaw locked. "Doesn't matter what it looks like. She's off-limits. Anyone touches her—even as a joke—they answer to me."

"Yeah?" Theo asked from across the room, arms folded. "You know we got your back, but are you sure about that?"

The air snapped between us as I gave him a curt nod. That

was the problem—I wasn't sure. Not about any of it. Mila was unraveling shit in me I didn't even know was still knotted. Stuff I'd buried deep enough I thought it couldn't hurt anymore. But now? It was rising—and I didn't know how to stop it.

Doubts crept in. Family loyalty ran deep, but something in my gut kept saying things weren't right.

Then there was the note. *She shouldn't be here. Fix it.*

It had to be Elise. I swore it was her handwriting, and it reeked of her flavor of petty. Especially lately, with desperation written all over her red matte lips. She wanted more—more status, more control, more of me. What we'd had wasn't a relationship. It was convenience. Temporary heat in the dark when I needed to forget. Nothing that had ever held weight.

She spun fantasies out of our past, dressing them up as promises I never made. She thought a ring down the line would save her. That being Mrs. King would buy her freedom from her father's leash and lock her into a lifetime of easy power.

She was delusional. We'd hooked up a few times before I'd met Mila and once at a party a few months ago. I wasn't sure why she kept pretending we were a thing when I'd made sure to clarify that it was a one-time event. Either way, I wasn't playing along. I'd outgrown the game. And I was done letting parasites feed off my name.

By lunch the next day, whispers started.

Elise worked fast—weaponizing truth and half-truths the way only someone with money and motive could. I caught pieces of it in the halls, fragments that hit harder because they weren't entirely false.

Mila, sleeping her way into Blackwood. Her mom, conning her way through the board. Social climbers in counterfeit couture, cashing in on reputations that weren't theirs to claim.

The worst part? I *knew* Mila's mom wasn't clean. I'd heard enough. Seen enough. I was aware she was seeing Principal Miller. Knew she'd charmed him the same way she had every man with a title. And yeah, maybe she took a little here and there. Maybe more. But Mila? Mila wasn't like her.

I saw Mila on campus, walking next to Avery, chin high, as though she wasn't breaking apart beneath the weight of the rumors. But I noticed the way her eyes blazed in challenge, her fingers curled into her palms as if she was preparing to strike out.

Avery played it cool—loyal as hell, ready to go feral if someone said the wrong thing. But even she couldn't stop the stares. The barely masked judgment in every sideways glance.

Outside the auditorium, I cornered Elise. She was laughing too loud with Tori and Nina, basking in the aftermath of her own chaos.

"Drop it," I said, voice low, threading steel through the warning.

She turned, all venom in silk. "You'll have to give me something in return, Luke."

I stared her down. "I wouldn't touch you again if you paid me."

Her smile thinned. "Careful who you piss off."

I walked. But I knew she wasn't done. She would never be done until I made it hurt to keep trying.

The guys would get the message. Anyone thinking about crossing my line would find themselves corrected. And if they didn't? I'd make an example.

That night, I stood outside the arena. Hands in my pockets. Heart pounding the way I'd just run sprints, even though I hadn't moved. I had no reason to be there. Except... I knew she would be inside. The light above the side entrance cast a pale glow over the ice, and even before I stepped in, I felt her.

Mila always used to haunt the art studio on the boardwalk. That was her place. Her escape. Her rebellion. Her mom hated it. Called it a hobby for the hopeless. Something that would land her on the streets instead of behind a desk with a six-figure salary.

But the rink? That was mine. Which meant it was familiar. Safe. And maybe… maybe she came here tonight because she wanted to feel tethered to something.

To me. She wouldn't admit it, but I felt it. That pull. That ache. Every movement deliberate but heavy with something she couldn't shake. Like she wasn't just clearing her head. She was *fighting* it. Trying to outrun the whispers. The past. Me.

I stayed for a while and watched her skate, needing an escape just as much as she did. The rink was quiet except for the scrape of her blades carving into ice. Her reflection shimmered beneath her, a second shadow. She moved with purpose, but it wasn't peace she was chasing.

It was distance. And it gutted me. Because I remembered what we had. I remembered the first time she let me pull her into the far corner, and she kissed me as if I was her only anchor. I remembered the way she used to wait for me here, hoodie swallowing her frame, nose red from the chilled air, fingers always cold.

Now she didn't wait for anyone. Not even me. And maybe that was my fault.

But as she moved—strong, precise, so goddamn alone—it was a bruise under my ribs. If she wasn't the villain in this story —what the fuck did that make me?

The chill clung to me even after I left the rink. I didn't let Mila see I'd been standing there. She moved as if nothing touched her. Watching her that way—so sure, so alone—it twisted something raw in my chest. I wanted to go to her. Drag her off the ice and demand answers she would never give me. Or maybe just press my hands to her hips, ground us both in something real for a second.

But I didn't. Because no matter what I wanted, I didn't trust her. Not anymore. Probably never again.

By the time I got to Jax's place, the bonfire was already raging. Flames licked the air, casting golden light over the lawn that sloped toward the lake. Sparks floated up like fireflies. The thud of bass pulsed from a speaker someone had set near a cooler, mixing with laughter, the crinkle of chip bags, the pour of the keg, and the hiss of popped beer tabs a select few had access to.

I dropped onto a log near the edge of the fire, elbows on my knees, hands threaded together. The guys were already halfway through a case, but the air was off. It was impossible not to feel the undercurrent. The shift.

Theo nudged my shin with the toe of his boot, a mischievous smirk curving his mouth. "You skip your nightly meditation skate or just miss being worshipped at school?"

I gave him a flat, borderline murderous look. "Keep running your mouth and I'll show you how cold that lake really is."

Jax grinned, leaned over, and tossed another log on the bonfire. "Nah, man. It's Mila. Girl shows up, and suddenly our fearless leader's short-circuiting. Never seen you this edgy."

"Shut the fuck up," I muttered, eyes locked on the fire.

But something in me was breaking down. Piece by piece. Mila had come back and taken every rule I'd built and lit them on fire. I didn't know what she was after. I couldn't tell if she was toying with me like her mom had played half this damn town—or if the hurt in her eyes was real.

It *felt* real. And that was the problem.

Chase wandered out of the shadows and over to us, hoodie pulled over his head, shoulders tense.

"What's going on with him?" I elbowed Jax.

"He hasn't said much all night. Not sure what it is." Jax cracked open a fresh beer. "Where's Avery?" he asked Chase, testing the waters.

Chase just shot him a glare that said everything.

"Just asking, man. You said you thought she would show and to watch out for her," Jax said, hands raised in mock surrender.

I let the silence stretch, eyes flicking over the rest of them. For a second—just one—it felt like before. Before secrets and threats and old ghosts returned with familiar eyes and a wicked tongue.

"I ever tell you guys," Jax started, tipping his head back to look at the stars, "I miss when our biggest problems were game day and who had better hair?"

I smirked, just a flicker. "You peaked sophomore year."

"Still have better stats than you this season," he shot back, grinning like he hadn't just lit a match.

"Keep dreaming." Laughter sparked around the fire. Easy. Surface-level. But it didn't last. Because none of this was easy anymore.

I glanced at Theo, who was nursing a beer and pretending not to pay attention. "Still screwing around with Tori?"

He blinked, caught off guard. "Why?"

I shrugged, ready to get to the heart of the problems going on during the day. "Because Elise and her crew don't do anything without an angle. And right now, she's gunning for Mila. That makes it our problem."

"You want me to spy?" His lips twitched. "That's cute. You going to pass me a note in class too?"

"I'm serious."

"So am I."

I leaned forward, voice low. "I don't care what you do with Tori. Just find out what Elise is planning. If she's got dirt. If she's targeting on Mila. I want to know first."

Jax let out a low whistle. "And here I thought you were just trying to get laid."

I ignored him. This wasn't about pride or jealousy. It was about control. About Mila. And the gnawing, gut-deep knowing that I didn't want anyone else touching her. Not Logan. Not anyone.

But every time I got close, there was another shadow. Her mom. Her past. The silence she wrapped around both. It all felt too close—a fire I hadn't put out and now couldn't stop from burning through everything.

But when she was on that ice… When she looked like the same girl who used to steal my hoodies and press freezing fingers to my neck just to watch me flinch?

I wanted her anyway. Even if she destroyed me. Especially if she did.

Jax passed me another beer. "You gonna keep staring at the fire, or are you gonna tell us what you're really thinking?"

I cracked the tab but didn't drink. "I'm thinking," I said, "that the next guy who tries to put hands on Mila is going to need dental reconstruction. Things have changed with her."

Theo snorted. "Duly noted."

"And I'm thinking Elise better pray she's smart enough to back off."

"Do you think she will?" Chase asked quietly.

I looked at him. Dead serious. "No. And when she doesn't… I'll manage it." Somehow, despite the "play nice" mandate from my father.

The guys didn't argue. They just nodded. Because they knew. This wasn't about romance. This was our territory, our rules.

CHAPTER FIFTEEN

MILA

I didn't want to be at the bonfire. Not after the day I'd had, or the calm I'd scraped together at the rink. But Avery showed up at my door with fire in her eyes and an attitude that screamed "get in the car or I'll drag you."

"You ditch on this and Elise wins," she'd said, arms crossed, every inch the general. "You want her to think you're hiding? That she got to you?"

Of course not. I knew the rules. Never let them see you bleed. But some nights? Bleeding in peace sounded like a luxury I couldn't afford.

"I just wanted a night to myself," I muttered, arms wrapped tight across my chest as I slouched in the back seat of Avery's friend's car. I didn't remember her name. Maybe it was Jasmine? She was too perky and too glittery, and her perfume made my head throb.

"I get it," Avery said, softer now. "But you can't keep letting them control the narrative."

God, I hated that word. As if this was all just a story being told by someone else—Elise with her shitty lies and cushy bank account—and I was stuck playing the villain in someone else's fairytale.

We pulled up to Jax's place and parked near a row of SUVs and overpriced cars. Laughter drifted from the back of the property. Flames flickered just past the tree line, clawing at the dark, orange and gold bleeding into the trees. I hesitated in the car.

Avery turned around, eyes too observant. "You good?"

No. Not even a little. "Yeah." I reached for the door handle. "Let's get this over with."

The air outside was cooler than I expected. It smelled of beer, smoke, and pine needles. The kind of scent that could almost be comforting if it weren't tied to high school politics and rich-kid power games.

We followed the path down toward the bonfire, the bass from someone's speaker vibrating through the ground. The second we stepped into the clearing, I regretted it.

Logan's eyes found me first. He was leaning against a tree with Elise and Nina flanking him, knockoff bodyguards at best, red Solo cup dangling from his hand. He tilted his head, a cruel smirk curving his thin mouth, the kind of grin that said he'd been waiting for me.

Elise's smile faltered for half a second, just long enough for me to see the panic flicker behind her perfectly lined eyes before she smoothed it over with a sip from her cup. She leaned closer to Logan, whispering something that made Nina snort— too loud, too fake. It was a performance. I'd already seen the crack in her composure.

The hair rose along the back of my neck as I felt his presence. *Luke.* I didn't look at him directly, but I didn't have to. I could feel the weight of his stare carving into the space between my shoulder blades. I lifted my gaze and met his head on. He didn't move, just stayed there, posted up with the other guys, royalty holding court over their private kingdom.

Avery led the way, weaving us through the crowd toward a group of girls I didn't know well. I kept my expression neutral, hiding the fact I was seconds from turning around and bolting.

"This is a power move," she whispered without looking at me. "Act the part."

I nodded. I got where she was coming from, respected it even. But tonight I was tired. And it wasn't only school, or Luke. It was the weight I came home to every night. It was also my mom. She'd been acting… off. Even for her.

She still left early, came home late, but now there was this added weight to her. Haunted eyes. Biting questions that came out of nowhere—Who are you talking to? How's school? Have you said anything about our past?

But never answers. Never context. She used to overshare. Used to crash on the couch beside me with takeout and spill stories from the office as if we were co-conspirators instead of mother and daughter. Back then, it felt like we were in this together. And she'd always make time for me. Now? She was a vault. And it scared me more than anything else.

The silence between us had thickened into something jagged —every word we didn't say cut deeper than the ones we used to shout or scream about. I knew she hated the rift, even if she wouldn't admit it—saw it in the way her gaze lingered on me too long, as though she was memorizing instead of mothering. Whatever she was protecting me from, it was pulling her further away.

The heaviness of it still clung to me as I followed Avery deeper into the clearing, the heat from the fire brushing my skin, as though it could burn away everything I didn't want to feel.

A keg sat near the trees, flanked by a cooler of canned drinks and a haphazard lineup of rum, vodka, and tequila with a few mixers thrown in as an afterthought. I grabbed a red Solo cup and filled it from the keg beer I didn't really want—just enough to take the edge off. Then I followed Avery and Jasmine to a spot far enough from the crowd to pretend I wasn't already counting down the seconds until I could leave.

The fire crackled behind us as I forced a smile, tapping my cup with Avery's and pretending the world wasn't spinning out beneath my feet. The music helped. So did the distraction of conversation, the lazy way Avery's friend Jasmine talked about her English teacher's tragic haircut, the bottle of something vaguely fruity that got passed around.

My guard dropped. Not all the way. But enough to breathe.

After I'd drained my subpar beer, I wandered toward the cooler to grab another drink, needing space for a second. The noise, the bodies, the looks—it was a lot.

That was when I felt it. That subtle shift in air pressure. The invasive presence behind me. I didn't even have to turn around to know someone unwanted was moving in on me.

"Didn't think you had the guts to show." Logan's nasally voice slithered against my ear.

I stiffened, closing the lid of the cooler slowly before turning to face him. "Back off."

He smiled. Too wide. "Come on. Don't be like that. Let's take a walk. Clear the air."

My grip on my still empty cup tightened. "I'm good right here."

His hand shot out, meaty fingers wrapping around my wrist.

His thin smile sharpened. "Don't make me ask twice."

I yanked my arm, twisting hard, just the way Mom's boyfriend Edwardo, who owned the gym, had taught me. His grip slipped, and I was free. "You touch me again," I growled, "you'll regret it."

He laughed as if I hadn't just meant every word. And then he wasn't laughing anymore. Because Luke was there. Between us in less than a breath.

His fist slammed into Logan's jaw, the crack echoing

through the trees. Logan staggered, spit flying, nearly toppling into the cooler.

Everyone froze. The party around us stuttered, the music still thumping, but now it felt off-beat—as though even the bass was holding every other breath.

Luke didn't flinch. He loomed over Logan, shoulders squared, eyes all ice and fury. "I warned you once. That was your shot. You touch her again, you don't walk away."

Logan's hand went to his jaw, blood blooming from his split lip. He looked around as if maybe someone would step in. But no one moved. Jax, Chase, Theo—they were already closing in behind Luke and me.

"You think I was kidding about laying hands on her?" Luke's voice cut like a blade.

Logan sneered through blood. "She's not yours. Not anymore. You made that clear at the start of the school year."

"Maybe not." Luke's voice was deadly calm. "But she sure as fuck isn't yours either."

Logan's fist clenched, his expression mutinous, and for one terrible second, I thought he might be dumb enough to swing. But he wasn't that stupid. He looked at the guys behind Luke. Read the room. Then he spat on the ground near my feet and stalked off toward the shadows.

I stood there, still vibrating with leftover adrenaline, my wrist throbbing where he'd grabbed me.

Luke turned to me, jaw clenched, eyes dark. "You okay?"

"I was handling it."

"Doesn't mean you had to do it alone."

I didn't answer. Didn't trust what would come out of my mouth. Because his voice—low, quiet, rough at the edges—cut straight through my defenses. Not cold, or cruel, just honest. And it undid me. That wasn't the Luke who'd iced me out since I came back. That wasn't the Luke who watched me skate and said nothing, because yeah, I'd clocked him there. That was someone else. Someone dangerous and familiar. And I didn't know what scared me more—that I didn't recognize him anymore. Or that I still wanted to.

CHAPTER SIXTEEN

LUKE

I didn't expect Mila to thank me. She stood there, eyes burning and chest rising as if she'd just been dragged through hell and dared someone to say something about it, and I knew we weren't done. This wasn't the place for the fight brewing in her expression. "Come with me." I kept my voice low.

She didn't move.

"Mila."

Her gaze flicked to where the other guys lingered near the fire, the glow painting them in gold and shadow. Chase and Jax were on alert, eyes scanning the party as though a threat might appear at any second. Theo? His attention had already shifted—locked onto Tori as she flicked her strawberry blond hair over her shoulder and the suggestive expression she shot his way.

I didn't wait for Mila's agreement. I turned and walked into the tree line behind at the edge of the party, down the sloped path toward the lake. I knew she would follow. She always did when it mattered.

It was quieter here, darker. The fire and noise behind us

faded to background static. Just the lake ahead, rippling in the moonlight, and the ache building beneath my ribs.

She finally stopped a few feet behind me.

"You don't get to do that," she snapped. "You don't get to swoop in and play fucking savior."

I turned to face her. "You wanted me to let him drag you off into the woods?"

"I had it under control."

"Bullshit."

"I did." She stepped closer, chin high. "I can handle anything these spoiled assholes throw at me. You forget who I am?"

"No," I said, too fast. "That's the problem. I remember exactly who you are."

That hit something in her—a flash of pain, quickly masked by anger. "Then stop pretending I need your protection," she bit out. "You lost the right to play hero from the moment I returned and you treated me like the enemy."

"Enemy, huh?" I crowded her. "Funny. You act as though I crowned you that. But let's not pretend you didn't come back swinging. From where I'm standing? You've worn the title since the day you left. And sure as hell when you came back."

I stepped farther in, just enough to make her lean back. Not enough to break the tension but to shift the air between us. My voice dropped. "Tell me something, Mila. That night—you could've called. Given one reason. Why didn't you?"

"You don't know what you're talking about." Her laugh was bitter. "Forget the past. Let's focus on the present. Specifically on tonight." She jammed her finger into my chest. "You can't hate me one second and then defend me the next."

I didn't answer. Didn't trust myself to. She nailed it. Straight through the ribs. No hesitation. I stood there, chest rising where her finger had jabbed me, every inch buzzing with words I couldn't say. Because she wasn't wrong. I *did* hate her. And I wanted her anyway.

The part that still ached when I looked at her—the part I buried under loyalty and legacy and whatever broken thing I called a heart—wanted her more now than ever.

She was so close I could feel the heat radiating off her skin. Sparks jumped in the space between us, taut and magnetic. One lean forward and I could kiss her. Claim her. Ruin every line we'd drawn. My pulse thundered. My hand twitched, caught between restraint and wanting to touch her—just once.

"I never said this made sense," I muttered, stepping back just enough to put some much-needed space between us. "But if you think I'll stand there and let some piece of shit put hands on you, you're even more delusional than I thought."

She blinked. "You're pissed that I won't let you play protector?"

"I'm pissed that I still give a damn." There. Out in the open.

Her mouth parted like she had a comeback locked and loaded—but nothing came. Just silence. Thick. Electric.

I watched her eyes shift, the anger fading slightly into something else. Confusion? Or maybe hurt. I could never tell with Mila. She kept her walls high.

"You're confusing, Luke," she whispered.

"You think I don't know that?" I ran my hands through my hair, hating the duality of my feelings for her. How everything was changing.

She didn't answer. Just stood there in the dark, the lake behind her glinting as if it held all the things we wouldn't say.

"I shouldn't feel anything when you're near. But I do. And I can't forget how it used to be." Her eyes searched mine.

"You really think I came back just to hurt you?"

"I don't know why you came back."

She looked away. There was too much between us—past feelings, hurt, and all the things left unsaid.

Through the tree line, the party swelled. A shout cut through the dull noise then laughter. The crinkle of a can crushed under someone's shoe. Elise's shrill voice again, weaving through the trees as if she was attempting to drive a wedge between us without even being here.

Mila sighed and took a step back toward the flicker of firelight. I followed without a word.

The path narrowed beneath our feet, pine needles crunching as we moved side by side. The glow of the bonfire grew stronger the closer we got, silhouettes sharpening from shadow to shape.

By the time we broke through the tree line, the sounds were clearer. Someone had turned the music louder. A group near the fire was arguing over a playlist. Elise's laugh carried above it all.

And then she saw us. Tori and Nina were with her as usual. But not for long. Theo moved in. He didn't say anything, just took Tori's hand and pulled her away with a look that said this conversation was over and what came next didn't require witnesses.

Nina smirked then eased closer to Chase. Elise ignored them as they disappeared into the woods. Her gaze locked on us before she took a step forward. But Chase and Jax moved into her path, casual on the surface, deliberate underneath. As if they hadn't just made it very clear this moment was off-limits.

Elise's mouth moved, full of venom. Jax just smirked and tipped his head, the picture of boredom. A grim smile tugged at my mouth, loving how they controlled the situation.

Mila noticed it too—her body eased just a fraction, finally able to breathe again.

"You done yelling at me?" I asked, voice lower now. Rougher.

She dragged her eyes back to mine. "Not even close."

"Didn't think so." I grinned, loving how feisty she was, even if we weren't anywhere close to a resolution.

She eased nearer to me, all fire and frustration wrapped in something heartbreakingly familiar. "You don't get to pick and choose when you care, Luke. I mean it. You don't get to label me an enemy, erase me, and then show up when it's convenient."

"I never erased you."

"Not true. When I came back, you made it crystal clear. You erased *us*."

The air stuck in my chest, heavier than it should've been. Even though it was partially bullshit. But she didn't want to bring the past into it? Fine. I wouldn't—this time. I closed the distance between us until there was barely an inch.

"Maybe," I admitted. "But don't act like we can rewind. You want real? Then don't show up half here and expect me to pretend that's enough."

Her breath caught.

I stepped in, drawn the way the tide reaches for the moon, close enough to feel her exhale on my skin. Her gaze flicked to my mouth then back to my eyes—raw, daring, conflicted. My hand brushed hers. Just a graze. Barely there. But it lit me up, a live wire—too hot, too close, too much. I leaned in more, not touching, just close enough that it felt like a decision.

Her breath hitched. So did mine. Her skin flushed, pupils blown wide, betraying how much she hated wanting this too. Her fingers twitched at her sides, caught between reaching for me or shoving me away. My lips hovered a breath from hers. One move. One second. And we'd tip over the edge.

But she didn't close the gap. Neither did I. The air between us pulsed—thick, buzzing, almost cruel. My chest was too tight. My skin, too itchy beneath my shirt. I wanted her with a goddamn ache I couldn't soothe.

Then she blinked, stepping back as though the ground between us was suddenly on fire. That almost burned more than the real thing ever could.

I kept going. "I don't trust you," I said again, slower this time, ready to drop a bomb so she was prepared for what was inevitable. "But I still want you. And I hate that more than everything else."

She didn't move. Neither did I. I could've touched her. Could've pulled her in and ruined both of us with a single kiss. But I didn't. Because nothing about us was simple. We were still suffering from wounds we hadn't even named yet.

The rustle of leaves behind us reminded me the world still turned, even when everything inside me had stopped.

"I should go." Her voice lacked conviction.

I nodded. "I'll walk you back to Avery."

She shook her head. "I'm not scared of Logan."

I gave her a small smile. "That's not why I'm offering."

She didn't argue. We walked back in silence, side by side but miles apart.

CHAPTER SEVENTEEN

MILA

Avery's and Jasmine's eyes were huge when Luke brought me over to them then left without a word. Avery opened her mouth to say something, but I shook my head, glancing at the crowd of people around us. She caught my message, and we found a spot away from the bonfire, off to the side and under a tree. Jasmine dropped to the ground, cracking open another drink. Avery perched on a log beside her.

"What was that?" Avery whispered.

I paused, searching for words. "Luke… I don't even…"

Jasmine shifted, concern flickering. "That looked serious. That was more than 'I hate you,' more than… what?"

Before I could shape an answer, my throat closed. Hearing him admit he still wanted me tilted my world, and I hated how much it mattered. So I shrugged. "That was Luke staking a claim, or some shit along those lines."

"A claim?" Avery frowned, gaze dark. "He totally went after Logan."

I snorted, forcing a laugh. "Territory bullshit. Two idiots circling a target."

Jasmine shook her head, pursing her lips, eyes contemplative. "He saved you, though. I saw how Logan had grabbed you."

My stomach flipped. "It's not what you think."

Avery straightened. "Luke wasn't messing around."

I rubbed my sore wrist—*thanks for that, Logan, you asshole.* Adrenaline still buzzing low in my veins. "Look—I need to go." I pulled my phone out and ordered a ride.

Avery touched my arm. "We'll drive you."

But I shook my head and waved toward the crowd of people, specifically Elise and her posse. "No—my ride's on the way. I'm done dealing with those idiots tonight." I forced out the words steady, cold. "And I have a headache."

They both nodded. Avery stood then pulled me in for a hug. "Call me later, okay?"

I managed a ghost of a smile. "Yeah." Then I moved through the crowd with purpose until I got to the street.

The ride back was quiet. A single text from Avery to remind me: "Call when you get home."

I didn't. I shot her a message I'd made it there instead.

At home, the porch light was too bright, exposing me. My mom was there, leaning against the doorframe still dressed in her work clothes from this morning, arms crossed.

"Where've you been?" She sounded calmer than I expected—more wary, weighing me instead of accusing.

My phone buzzed again. I glanced: a single missed message from her, the time stamp from a few minutes ago. I stuffed it in my pocket. "Out with friends."

"Friends?" She stepped inside, voice clipped. "You didn't answer your phone. I was worried."

I laughed, bitter. "You don't check in all hours of the night—why start now?" I pulled my phone back out and showed her the time stamp of her message. "So worried. I just got this. Where the hell have *you* been?"

Her lips compressed into a line. "Don't do that."

"Fine." I leaned against the door and crossed my arms over my chest. "I heard a rumor—about you and Principal Miller."

She froze. Then brushed it off with a shrug. "I've seen Warren a few times. It's not a big deal."

"Yeah, it kinda is. Seems I'm getting discounted tuition, special treatment. Sound about right?"

Her face flickered—anger, hurt, something like regret. "Do you understand how hard I'm working? How much I sacrifice for your future?"

I shoved loose strands from my face. "I know you promised me that moving back to this town would set me up for the future. But it doesn't seem that way. You've been acting weird. We never talk anymore. You're secretive. And half the time you're gone."

Her shoulders drooped, weariness creeping in as if it physically hurt her to carry this. "You thought we moved back because the job was too good to pass up, right?"

"Didn't we?"

She laughed once, bitter and low. "Yeah, that was kinda the plan. But plans don't mean shit when the savings dry up faster than you expect. Rent here—even in this dump—is outrageous. That used car for you wiped us out. Independence isn't free. Tuition at Blackwood Academy?" Her voice tightened. "It's brutal. The discount helps. And the principal?" Her mouth twisted. "He's not dangerous. There's no real risk there. He knows the score. He's not a complete idiot."

Her voice cracked. "I've been holding everything together. The past year was rough. We burned through our savings. Bookkeeping at the gym—it didn't pay much."

"Rent was free because you—because of Edwardo." The words slipped out on their own. My skin heated beneath her stare. There was history between those two. We'd stayed with him before, when I was younger. Mom never really got into it much, and I'd let her get away with it because I liked him. He was good people.

She winced. "We needed a place to stay."

Then her face shuttered, and for a moment, I saw my own future in here—the same hardness, only older. I didn't know how to change the trajectory of my life.

"You know the deal. Stop pretending you don't know what I do for our survival, to make a better life for us."

But I did know. She didn't always like the guys she was with. Mom was smart; she had to be to do the bookkeeping gigs she easily got. The problem was, she had me at seventeen, never got to go to college, and her religious family kicked her out as soon as they found out she was pregnant with me, and whoever my dad was didn't stick by her. She'd been hustling ever since to provide for us.

I had to look away; the dig at her was eating me alive. The silence pressed in so loud I could hear my own heartbeat.

"You're getting opportunities I never had."

I flinched. She was right. She was there for me in so many ways, the past few weeks aside. The truth was, I missed her. She wasn't just my mom; we were friends. I wanted to collapse. I willed away the tears that pricked behind my eyes. "Nothing's been the same since we got back. That's what I'm upset about, not the principal."

She glanced away, her shoulders curving in. "I'm trying, Mila. This place isn't the easiest for me either, but you'll get into any school you want with scholarships if we can tough it out. I want you to have more than I ever did."

"And I'm tired." My voice broke. I should apologize, but I was so damn tired of whatever was going on with her, with this town, with Luke... I just needed a break. "I'm tired of wondering where you are, what's going on, and if we're going to have to leave in the middle of the night again."

It wasn't just the fight with her. It was him. Luke. The way we stood there by the lake, barely breathing, one moment from falling into old patterns. His lips had been too close. I should've pushed him away. Should've turned my back and walked, but everything in me tilted toward him anyway. Instead, I'd lingered as if I wanted it. That almost-kiss? It gutted me worse than if he'd followed through. Because almost meant we still could. And I wasn't sure I could survive that again.

Mom turned back toward me, her eyes wide. "I'm sorry." She hesitated. "Please—don't make this about leaving. We need to make the best of things, no matter what. I'm doing what I can, and… I'll try to be around more."

"Don't worry about it," I whispered, over the conversation and the wreckage that lay between us. I stepped around her to the hallway.

My room looked the same. Impersonal. Clean. Nothing on the walls, no photos on the shelves. Just a slate bedspread, clothes stacked in the closet, and my art supplies hidden like contraband. If I so much as sketched near Mom, she got twitchy —as though my craving for something uncertain made her skin itch. She was talented once. I remembered watching her draw when I was small. But she shelved it. Traded charcoal for spreadsheets. Said numbers made sense. Said they paid the bills.

I got it—why she hated it. Why she wanted something safer for me. But art fed a part of me nothing else could touch. Since coming back, I hadn't stepped foot inside the boardwalk studio. Couldn't. The place would still smell of turpentine and salt air, and if I let myself think too long, I could feel the grainy texture of the canvas under my fingers. I'd left pieces there—an oil portrait of a girl with rain in her eyes, charcoal renderings of the pier from memory, one sketch of Luke I'd never admit was him. Not sure if any of it still hung. Not sure I wanted to know. I hadn't dared bring them home. My chest tightened just thinking about it. I would go back. I knew that much. Sooner than I wanted. Sooner than I was ready for.

I collapsed on the bed, staring at the ceiling. My head throbbed, a relentless drumbeat, every thump a reminder of Luke's words echoing in my skull.

I still want you. His confession pulsed in my veins: *I don't trust you... but I still want you.*

A riptide of emotions seized me—relief, dread, longing, fury. I realized I was more broken than I thought.

And it wasn't just because he still wanted me—or even because I wanted him. It was because despite everything—my mom's issues, the rumors still swirling—I might let him in again. Might fall all over, knowing full well the cost.

I exhaled sharply. I mulled it over, heart heavy with everything I couldn't undo—and everything I couldn't let go. The night stretched ahead, and I wasn't sure if I would be able to sleep.

CHAPTER EIGHTEEN

LUKE

Flames leapt higher as someone tossed on another log, sparks spiraling into the night. Jax, Chase, and I lounged in a secluded section of the grounds. A few guys hovered nearby, but no one crossed into our corner. Tonight, the east side of the fire was ours.

Jax had brought a case of beer from the house for us, his parents off in Europe for a week or so. I sipped what was only my second, and last, beer of the evening. My gaze was fixed on the flames, but my mind was tracking where I'd seen Mila slip into the shadows, how easily she moved through the crowd only to disappear along the trail that led to the street. I'd barely stopped myself from going after her—again. The pull I felt toward her was nearly impossible to resist.

Movement drew my attention just as Theo emerged from the trees, shirt clinging, hair mussed in a way that said Tori had been there. He dropped next to me, breathing hard.

"We good?" he asked, nodding at the rest of our crew.

"Always," I answered flat.

Chase glanced between us but directed his question to Theo. "Find out anything?"

Theo met my gaze. "Tori says Elise is pissed. Wants Mila gone. Says she thinks Mila's stepping on her turf. Nothing we didn't already know."

Jax scoffed. "Pretty sure Elise's turf stops at her dad's wallet. It doesn't stretch to the rink."

"No," I said, voice tight.

Theo grabbed a beer and cracked it open. "She's under the impression you two are getting back together."

"Whatever she thought we had—it was nothing. If she made it into more, that's on her." My words were met with nods.

"You sure she won't try something?" Jax leaned forward, elbows resting on his knees. "Not just rumors. Real shit—what could've gone down tonight if you hadn't intervened?"

Across the clearing, Elise stood with Nina and Tori near the makeshift drinks table, her arms crossed and her posture rigid. Firelight danced across her expression, but it did nothing to soften the sharp set of her jaw. Her gaze locked on us—on me— with a quiet fury that promised she wasn't done. But she didn't move closer. None of them did. This part of the party was ours, and they weren't invited.

I met Jax's stare. "Elise is jealous. Narcissistic. But after tonight, she should be smart enough not to mess with Mila in the same way again."

A flicker of doubt crossed Jax's face. Not about Elise—about me and Mila, and the way everything was shifting. Protection. Possession. The line between them was razor-thin, and he knew it. His gaze drifted to Avery, where she sat laughing with Jasmine, as if this night hadn't split anything open.

Chase's eyes narrowed, but he said nothing.

I watched Jax's face shift—the way he looked at Avery, the hesitation in his posture. How he seemed to soften whenever he sought her out, yet not once had he made a move. When he did, things would be dicey.

I shifted on the log. The fire crackled. My chest tightened.

Because despite everything—Elise's bullshit, our tangled past, the secrets that jammed between us—I couldn't ignore how raw I felt about Mila.

Protect her. That part came easy. Instinctive. The rest—what I felt when she looked at me as if she still knew me, as if the past hadn't scorched everything between us—that was harder to ignore. I didn't trust her. I might never again. But I still craved her in a way that made everything else feel peripheral.

"Elise is smart. Strategic." I kept my voice loud enough for only us to hear. "She's already used Logan as her puppet to get to Mila. We need to keep an eye out for anything else she could try."

Jax rubbed his chin. "So we keep our eyes open. Make an example if needed."

"Exactly," I said, still staring into the fire. "Anyone lays a hand on Mila again, they'll feel it."

A beat passed. Just the fire crackling, the low bass of music humming across the yard.

Chase shifted. "So what's the plan? You bringing her back in? Like before?"

"No." I kept my voice even. "Not like before."

Theo's brow rose. "But she's under our protection?"

"She is," I said. "No one touches her. But she doesn't get my trust back. Not after she left."

Jax leaned forward, elbows on his knees. "So she's not one of us… but no one else touches her either."

"Exactly."

Chase gave me a look. "You really think you can keep that line clean?"

I didn't answer right away. Because no—there was nothing simple about this. "I'll handle it," I growled. "Whatever this is, it's mine to carry."

Jax clapped a hand on my shoulder, solid and wordless.

Silence stretched again, until Jax cut through it, eyes glinting. "So what now?"

I glanced toward the tree line where I'd told her the truth. "She came back."

"And?"

"I still want her." The words tasted of blood in my mouth.

Jax smirked, but it didn't quite reach his eyes. "Then what the hell are you doing sitting here?"

I didn't smile, just drained the last of my beer and crushed the can in one hand.

"I'm not done with her."

Chase stood, brushing ash from his jeans—leftovers from embers that had burned out and drifted down. "Just don't forget who she used to be."

"I haven't," I said.

He walked off without another word. Jax looked at me, like he was waiting.

"Where you going?" he asked.

My eyes tracked toward the fire's edge, where I'd seen her last.

"Nowhere," I muttered. But I was lying. Mostly to myself. I wanted to go to Mila, but I wouldn't go to her, not yet.

Because no matter how much I hated what she'd done—I still wanted her. And that want wasn't a choice anymore. It was a curse.

CHAPTER NINETEEN

MILA

The bell rang, signaling the end to second period, echoing down the hall as I ducked into the bathroom between classes. Fluorescent lights buzzed overhead, casting a sterile glow against the mirror. I slipped into a stall then when straight to the sink to wash my hands, avoiding my reflection. I didn't want to see if there were half-moons hanging beneath my eyes. I was tired of everything—my mom, Luke, the bullshit games with him and his crew, and Elise's posturing.

The bathroom door opened. I didn't need to look—I felt the malice oozing into the space before I saw them. They came into view in the mirror. I sighed then grabbed a few paper towels.

Elise. Flanked by Nina and Tori. Three shadows under the fluorescent lights.

Elise leaned in, pressing me against the sink's edge. "You're stepping where you shouldn't." She pushed her straight black hair over one shoulder, chin tilted, cutting as glass. Her eyes narrowed into menacing slits.

I shut off the tap, wadded the towel up in my hand and taunted, "Oh? Please elaborate."

Nina crossed her arms, taller than Elise, looming behind her.

Tori hovered by the door, shoulder pressed to the frame, eyes flicking between us. She didn't concern me. Not yet. She was more of a sidekick, and her impact with the group lessened if Theo was around. I was counting on that to influence her to walk a careful line between Elise and the guys.

Elise jabbed a finger under my collarbone, pushing me back. "Charity projects like you don't get legacy."

Every nerve fired up. I swatted her hand off me before she could press further. My stance was rigid, ready to pivot if she wanted a fight. I let my lip curl. "Do tell."

"Stay out of what doesn't belong to you," Nina hissed.

"Ahh, I see. You think you're… special?" I mocked. "Here's your permission slip to try to make me stay in my place." I wanted them to make a move. I was itching for a physical fight, but these three? They didn't have it in them. Or, at least, I didn't think they did. "What you're saying isn't anything new. You're tired. Boring. Not worthy of listening to."

"If you weren't so dense, I wouldn't have to repeat myself. So listen up, charity case, and hear my words as law," Elise sneered. "The guys? They're ours. And Luke is mine."

"Excuse me?" Laughter bubbled up, dark and sarcastic. "Does he know this? Good luck with that one—you want a leash? Get a dog."

Nina smirked. "You don't know him. Don't pretend you do."

Funny about that—I knew him in ways Elise only wished she did. My body heated at even the hint of that thought before I shoved it back in the vault in my mind. Now wasn't the time.

Tori chewed her lip. I caught her eyes, and she blinked, smoothing her expression out, puffing up her shoulders, masking herself in hive mentality, pretending she agreed.

Elise jutted out her chin. "He doesn't need someone damaged the way you are. Broken. Used and discarded." She leaned close. "Guys like Luke? They stick to their own, and that isn't you."

I leaned against the sink, slow and steady, arms crossed. "You came at me with words. Opinions. Do you expect me to flinch?" My mouth curved—no humor in it. "I'd have to care about your opinion, or that of strangers for that to work."

Elise's nostrils flared. Nina stiffened beside her, that smug expression slipping just a fraction.

I straightened, dropped my arms to my sides, letting my voice cut low and lethal. "As for Luke? Been there, done that. He's all yours."

Tori looked away, her posture faltering for half a second before she caught herself and mirrored Nina's stance.

Elise didn't flinch, but her silence was louder than anything she could've said.

I gave them one last look. "Strange—you keep calling me beneath you, but you sound terrified."

Elise's bloodred lips thinned. "We'll see how long you keep running your mouth when things fall apart."

I tilted my head. "Can't wait."

They turned, Tori yanked the door wide, and the three of them stalked out, heels echoing off the tile. The door slammed behind them, the dull thud vibrating through the space. The silence they left behind didn't rattle me—it charged me. One thing was for sure; I wasn't bored.

I waited until their footsteps faded down the hall before glancing at my reflection. My eyes shone, and color highlighted my cheeks—I looked alive. A devious grin curved my lips, and I inhaled deeply. My heart thundered, but my hands were steady. They wanted fear; I gave them fire. With that last thought, I exited the bathroom into the hallway.

My mouth pressed into a line when I caught sight of Chase's arm draped over Avery's shoulders, protective as ever. Fraternal twins, they didn't look identical, but they were both striking, blond, and blue eyed. His features were more chiseled to her heart-shaped face.

Tightness spread through my shoulder blades to my stomach. Where he was, the others weren't far—and I was in no mood for another run-in with Luke. It was hard enough when I'd walked into calculus and witnessed him run his hand through his hair, in frustration, his shirt raising an inch for a glimpse of rock-hard abs. I had to check to make sure I wasn't drooling over the sight. Instead, I was avoiding him. Nothing good could come of us acting on what he'd confessed at the bonfire.

Avery's head snapped up when she noticed me, her gaze crawling over my face. She jerked to a stop, forcing her brother to as well. "What happened?"

Chase gave me a once-over, grunted, then left without another word. Avery ignored him, her focus still locked on me.

I shrugged, doing my best to shake off the adrenaline still humming through me. "Bathroom drama."

Jasmine skidded to a halt beside Avery, tawny eyebrows raised.

"They cornered you, huh?" Avery narrowed her eyes. "What'd Elise say?"

I sighed. "Charity case... stepping on their turf... they want Luke back."

Jasmine's lip curled. "Annoying."

Avery's eyes softened. "You okay?"

"I'm fine." Only I wasn't. I was spoiling for a fight but also sick of the drama. "Can we just... not do the gossip thing today?"

She pursed her lips. "I get it, but you need to know that Elise is tracking your every move. She overheard something last night."

Last night—the almost-kiss and the charged tension between Luke and me. I suppressed a shiver at the memory. "I'm not the same girl she thinks she knew," I said with more heat than I intended.

"She's dangerous."

Not really. Not to me. And not compared to what molded me into who I was the past year. "I can handle it."

Lunch was blessedly uneventful. I even made it through three classes before the rumble began. Whispers—dozens of them drifting through the space. It was laughable. No one mentioned the almost-kiss, as I was sure Elise wouldn't want anyone believing he was interested in me. Among the top three were Mila was crying after the bonfire, Luke told her to leave town, and she threw herself at him, and he rejected her.

I didn't give any of the rumors power. None of it bothered me. I think if they knew he'd almost kissed me, I might have felt something. Instead, I didn't stop in the hall on the way out. Just kept walking. Or I'd planned to walk out before Avery fell into step beside me before I reached the parking lot.

She bumped her shoulder into mine. After glancing around to see who was near us, her smile fell. "I heard something today."

"Yeah, so did I. My favorite rumor was Luke telling me to leave town."

"I'm not talking about from Elise and her rumor train. I talked to my brother. He said something about Luke and you looking pretty close, intense and not in a fighting way, while you were talking. You sure you're good?"

My throat closed. I hesitated. "It didn't mean anything." My voice was flat. "Letting him anywhere near me was a mistake."

She glanced at me, judgment soft. "You sure, Mila?"

I offered her a small, tight smile. "I'm sure," I told her, before escaping to my car and home. Of course, Mom wasn't there. But she wouldn't be, not when it was still during work hours. I exhaled a relieved breath the second my door closed. My backpack fell with a thud at my feet, and I flopped onto my bed where the almost-kiss replayed in my mind, a film stuck on one frame.

I rolled to my side, eyes landing on the nightstand drawer where my sketchbook hid. The urge to pull it out—to catch that frame before it faded, the sharp cut of his jaw, the heat in his eyes—slammed into me hard enough to ache.

But sketching him would make it real. Permanent. Dangerous.

So I stayed frozen, denying myself the only outlet that ever gave me more than clawing through survival.

His lips. Close. His breath on mine. How close he came. *We still could.* I shook it off, cold water on my skin. I couldn't let myself sink again. Because if I let myself fall—I might never find the ground.

I closed my eyes, willing the heat behind them to cool. Wanting him was walking barefoot through broken glass— every step closer just promised blood.

CHAPTER TWENTY

LUKE

The locker room stank—stale sweat and unspoken grudges clinging to the walls. I yanked my shirt over my damp hair and shut my locker with more force than necessary. It echoed, but no one called me on it.

Mila hadn't said a word when I walked her back to Avery at the bonfire. Just that unreadable look in her eyes—uncertain if I was her enemy or her last line of defense. Hell, maybe I didn't know either.

"King." Jax tossed a rolled-up sock at my chest. "You planning to glare at the lockers all day or join the rest of us in pretending this place doesn't suck?"

I caught the sock midair. "Funny."

Chase leaned against the bench across from me, arms folded. "You look like shit."

"Thanks. You're glowing as always."

Theo snorted. "Seriously though. You gonna tell us what's up or keep brooding until you combust?"

I shrugged. "Nothing's up."

"I call bullshit," Jax muttered.

He wasn't wrong. Practice had been brutal. I'd pushed

harder than anyone—faster drills, heavier hits, sharper checks. Coach didn't say much, just narrowed his eyes and let me work it out on the ice. He knew better than to ask. Everyone did. Except my crew.

I dropped onto the bench and leaned forward, elbows on my knees, voice low. "Logan couldn't take his eyes off her in gym class."

Jax swore. Chase's posture went still.

"Something's brewing." Elise's smirk when I walked past her told me more than she probably wanted me to know.

"He touch her again?" Chase asked.

"No." My voice was flat. Final. "He won't."

We all knew that wasn't the end of it, though. Not with Elise whispering in ears and Logan acting as if he had something to prove. The two of them were toxic as hell. And Mila was their favorite target because she didn't flinch. She made them look small just by standing tall. And because Elise thought Mila had something that should've been hers—me.

"I think it's time we do something," Jax said.

I looked up. "It is. What are you thinking?"

"We need to put Logan in his place." Jax's eyes narrowed. "Publicly."

That was what I'd already planned to do, and vocalized enough.

"Too messy," Chase countered. "That's what Elise wants— make Mila look like the drama."

I studied Chase. He wasn't concerned for Mila—it was his sister. He was worried Avery would be a target. Or worse, collateral damage. We would never let that happen. Especially Jax. Whoever had hurt Avery last year left scars we all carried. Chase most of all. Avery had been a shell back then, and her brother never forgot it.

"We're already in it," I said. "Might as well stop pretending we're not."

Theo crossed his arms. "Tori said Elise's been asking around about Mila's old schools. Trying to dig something up."

"Let her," I said. "There's nothing there." The words came out easy, automatic. But memory flickered—Mila in calculus, head bent, sketching in the margin of her notes instead of listening. Not doodles. Real drawings. Beautiful, precise, and alive. I'd caught myself staring longer than I should have. Elise could dig all she wanted. The girl she was looking for—the one she thought Mila had to be—wasn't who I'd seen in those lines.

Chase shook his head. "Doesn't matter. Truth isn't what she cares about—it's the story she can spin."

I didn't respond. He was right. Elise never needed facts. Just an audience.

Jax leaned back, kicking his feet up. "We've been letting this ride too long. Time to turn the game on them."

Theo looked at me. "You're the captain. You make the call."

Silence stretched. The kind that presses on your ribs and makes you feel as though you're about to drown. I ran a hand through my hair. "We need to be smart. Logan's stupid enough to mess up on his own—we just need to give him enough rope."

Chase raised an eyebrow. "You want to bait him?"

"Not bait," I said. "Just… give him an opportunity to reveal himself."

Jax grinned. "Now that's the Luke I know."

"Keep it quiet. Subtle," I added. "As for Elise, we let her think she's ahead. That's when she'll get sloppy."

Theo cracked his knuckles. "Tori hears anything, I'll know."

"And if Logan makes another move?" Chase asked.

I didn't hesitate. "Then I break his fucking face."

The others nodded. Our mutual understanding was forged through years of blood, blades, and silent loyalty.

As we grabbed our gear and headed toward the exit, my phone buzzed in my pocket. A text from Drew.

Family dinner. Tomorrow. Don't bail this time.

My jaw locked. Another performance in the empire they pretended was a family. My parents didn't play house—they ran it as a joint operation, cold and calculated. Love never factored into the equation. Power did. Image did.

I didn't respond to Drew's message.

As we stepped out into the crisp evening air, I glanced toward the rink—empty now, lights off, but still charged with memory. I told myself this wasn't really about Mila. That I was just protecting the team. Keeping the power where it belonged —with us. That Elise and Logan were problems I needed to solve. But even I didn't believe that anymore.

CHAPTER TWENTY-ONE

MILA

The restaurant buzzed with weekend noise—ice rattling in plastic cups, bursts of laughter, music pouring from the speakers like static. This was the place to be seen. And I hated that I agreed to come.

Avery waved me over from the corner booth, already halfway through her milkshake. Jasmine leaned back in the vinyl seat, her phone glowing. Margie walked over to the booth with a cheeseburger and fries in a red basket lined with checkered paper. She slid in, and they resumed their conversation. They looked relaxed. Normal.

I slid in beside them, faking the ease I didn't feel.

The booth smelled like salt and grease, ketchup packets sticking to the Formica. Their chatter blurred into the background noise. My eyes snagged on the paper placemat beneath my drink. A doodle had already bled across the corner—some other restless hand leaving swirls and lines.

My fingers itched to steal the pen from Jasmine's purse. To sketch the way the light caught Avery's laugh or the sharp cut of Margie's hands when she talked. Instead, I curled my hands in my lap. If I started, I might not stop. And Avery's friends weren't ready to see the real me—the one who saw the world in lines and shadows instead of labels and brands.

Margie was mid-rant, manicured nails dancing in the air. "So I found these jeans—limited drop, ultra high-rise, stupid expensive, obviously. I bought two sizes just in case. The smaller one's my motivation, don't judge."

Avery laughed. "Only you would spend that much on denim you can't even breathe in yet."

"I'll breathe after I look amazing," Margie shot back, sipping her lemonade with a wink.

Jasmine rolled her eyes. "She's dragging us to the boutique on Cypress tomorrow. Claims they just restocked."

"Post-brunch beach trip tomorrow too," Margie added, flashing her phone screen. "This bikini needs sunlight and sin. Preferably both."

I smiled, pretending I belonged.

We'd lived in nice places. Stayed in fancy homes when Mom's boyfriends had money. But they weren't legacy. Not this level. Not deep pockets with deeper secrets.

Fifteen minutes later, I excused myself, needing a break. Too much pretending.

The bathroom was down a narrow hallway, tucked past the arcade claw machines and a side exit. I took my time washing my hands, letting the water scald and numb in equal measure.

As I pushed the bathroom door open, voices leaked down the hallway—hushed and familiar. Elise's. I froze, catching her mid-sentence.

"...doesn't matter how broke they look—Mila's mom always finds a way to cash out."

It crashed through me like a gut punch. Not because she was wrong. But because it was too close to the truth.

She was talking about me. It couldn't be more obvious. I stepped out fully then, slow and on purpose, making sure she saw me. Her gaze flicked up, mouth curling as if she'd been waiting all along. Nina loitered behind her, smug. Tori lingered near the hall entrance, half-turned like she wanted to bolt.

"You and I should talk," Elise said, voice venom, saccharine and glass. "Girl to girl."

I leaned against the wall, arms crossed, casual mask in place, refusing to give her the satisfaction of a reaction.

She cocked her head, dark hair gleaming under the too-bright overhead light. "Heard you've been… busy."

I raised a brow. "You stalking my schedule now?"

Nina smirked. Tori shifted her weight but said nothing.

Elise's smile thinned. "I just think someone should remind you—your mom's history has a way of catching up."

My blood went cold. What exactly was she talking about? Why we left? Or something else?

She stepped closer, just enough to push into my space. "Men. Money. The way she leaves both behind a little lighter." Her gaze dragged over me. "Ring a bell?"

That. I caught her drift, and it wasn't surprising what she'd found out. Even so, I didn't move. I wouldn't give her the satisfaction.

"Let me guess," she went on, voice hushed. "Luke's next. Rising star. Heir apparent. Whole town already half-bowing to his last name. Bet she's real proud."

My jaw clenched. "You think I'm after Luke for his money?"

"I think you learned from the best." She smiled, all teeth. "Like mother, like daughter."

I was expecting something along those lines. "Really? Then why not go after his *older* brother? Isn't he already working at the company? Seems like the smarter target, if I was into power plays."

Elise's eyes glittered. She didn't answer right away, just tilted her head, lips curling into something secretive. "You would think. But some stars burn out before they even get the crown."

I stilled. Not because I gave a damn about her digs, but

because that line wasn't random. It sounded too specific. Too pointed. As if she knew something about Drew—something recent. The way she said it, too smooth and smug... it wasn't just gossip. It was a warning shot. Something was going down, and either she was behind it—or already watching it implode.

"You think you've got history with Luke? You're nothing new, Mila. I had him before you—and after. You weren't the first, and you sure as hell weren't the last."

Her words sliced through before I could brace, sharp enough to scrape bone. A hundred images I didn't want—Luke with her, Luke letting her close—flashed and burned before I shoved them down. My jaw ached from holding still. My face gave her nothing, even while my stomach twisted. I wouldn't give her the win.

Of course she would use him. Drag him between us like a bomb ready to explode. That was her game—make me bleed.

The silence stretched. Then she stepped back, tone sweet again. "Just thought you deserved a heads-up. Would hate to see history repeat itself."

Nina followed her down the hall. Tori stayed back a second longer—eyes flickering to me, almost uncertain—before falling in line.

I waited until their heels faded down the corridor before I breathed again. Their steps faded. So did my pulse. Elise wanted me rattled, but all she managed was to confirm one thing—she was digging. Hard.

I pushed the door open and headed back to the booth on autopilot.

Avery looked up the second I slid into my seat. "You okay?"

I offered a tight smile. "Yeah. Bathroom line was just long." The lie slid out easily, but the press of her lips said she didn't buy it.

She didn't press, but her gaze tracked me as the door chimed behind us. I didn't have to look—again. I swear I had a sixth sense for certain people. Then I felt it—Luke stepping into the restaurant. Jax. Chase. Theo. All of them moving as if they owned the place.

Part of me wanted to lean in, let him know Elise was chasing a new thread. But the memory of his words at the bonfire stopped me cold. He didn't get to say those things and expect me to fold. Screw that. Elise? I would handle her on my own.

Avery and Jasmine glanced toward the door, but Margie stayed glued to her phone. I didn't bother checking to confirm I was right.

I just picked up my cup and took a slow sip. Because whatever campaign Elise had started—it wasn't over. And if she thought she could intimidate me? She was out of her damn mind.

CHAPTER TWENTY-TWO

LUKE

The second I stepped into the restaurant, I regretted coming. It was loud in a way that grated—too many people, too much forced laughter. It was the popular hangout, and we came because it had the best burgers around. I could do without some of the crowd.

Chase bumped my shoulder with his. "Don't look now. Elise and her minions are here."

Not what I need. I didn't answer and instead made my way to the front. It didn't take long to put our food order in and pick it up from the counter.

We found our usual table in the back—round, semi-private, but still obnoxiously on display. Theo sprawled into one of the corner seats, already halfway through a basket of fries. Jax slid in beside him, pushing at Chase until he moved. Chase flipped him off and dropped into the seat next to me.

Tori showed up a beat later, tossing her jacket on the back of Theo's chair before climbing onto his lap, claiming it as if it was hers by birthright. He didn't even blink, just wrapped an arm around her waist and kept chewing.

Nina was across the room, elbow propped against the bar,

laughing at something some lacrosse bro was saying. The guy leaned in close. She didn't lean away.

I kept my head down until I caught the edge of a familiar intoxicating laugh. My eyes snapped up. And there she was— Mila.

Tucked into a booth across the room, back straight, hair loose around her shoulders and tumbling down her back. Her fingers danced around the edge of her pop, and she smiled at something the guy standing in front of her table said. I recognized him from the football team. Simon. He was a wide receiver. Decent guy. Didn't mean he was good enough for Mila.

Jealousy cracked through me as merciless as a whip.

She looked up as Simon sat next to her, Avery and her friends chatting away like there wasn't going to be an explosion of detrimental proportions in zero point two seconds. And for a moment—just one—our eyes locked. The world went quiet. Her smile faltered.

Then she blinked, looked away, and leaned slightly toward Simon. Her shoulder brushed his as she reached for her drink.

Jax snorted beside me. "Guess she's not too broken up about you."

I shoved past him and took the seat farthest from where she sat, my back angled just enough that I could still see her in the mirror behind the bar. I told myself it was coincidence. Even I didn't believe that.

Elise slid into the chair beside me, her bracelet clinking against the table, a deliberate mark announcing her arrival. Always performing. Always demanding attention. She followed my line of sight, her body bracing momentarily when she realized who I was watching.

"Didn't think we would see *her* here." Her voice dripped honey-laced poison.

"What the fuck do you want Elise?" I glared before glancing

at the menu board above the counter even though I wasn't planning on ordering anything more.

She leaned into my side, her red manicured nails grasping onto my bicep. "I'm just saying. I didn't realize they let strays in."

I didn't answer. Some of the guys got up, bringing back more food. I continued to stew in my seat, my gaze locked on Mila's table while Elise fluttered around me, a buzzing nuisance I couldn't swat away.

As soon as the guys were deep in a conversation about our next game, she leaned in. "You know my dad keeps saying it's time we make things official."

I looked at her sideways. "Pretty sure your dad's idea of official is a press release."

She smiled, calculating and practiced. "Just think about it. Your family. My family. Top two names in Blackwood."

I smirked. "King Enterprises still outranks Dunn Investments by a few zeros. You sure your dad wants that comparison?"

"Power shifts fast—you know that." She tapped her manicured nails against the table, each click deliberate. "But alliances last. And I'm the right one."

"You're not pitching a merger."

"No," she said, turning her head slightly, letting her hair fall over her shoulder. "I'm offering you security when things go sideways."

I raised a brow. "This your idea of flirting?" She couldn't know shit, but regardless, I was going to have to pass this little threat over to either Drew or my dad. Because in these types of situations, there would always be solidarity in family.

"This is my idea of reality." Her voice dropped lower. "You and Mila? That's chaos. We're certainty."

A beat stretched between us. I laughed under my breath. "You mean convenient."

"I mean inevitable." Her nails clicked again. "And I can make the noise around her disappear. All of it. The rumors, the whispers, the shit people are too polite to say to her face… or aren't. I can end it with a look."

I stared at her. "You know how to start it too, though, don't you?"

She shrugged. "Depends on whether I'm protecting something… or breaking it."

Her hand settled possessively on my thigh under the table.

Across the room, Mila nudged Simon. He stood as she grabbed her bag then slid out of the booth. Her head turned just enough to catch Elise's hand still resting on me. Something flickered across her face.

Pain? Anger? Disgust? She looked away before I could tell. I shoved Elise's hand off me.

"Don't touch me."

She tilted her head, trying to disguise a flicker of unease. "You're not mad I said it. You're mad I'm right."

"I'm annoyed you think you matter."

Elise's smile didn't fade. "You'll see, Luke. When everything else falls apart, I'll still be here."

I pushed back from the table and stood. She didn't try to stop me.

Outside, the air was cooler, denser than I expected. Thick clouds strangled the last of the light, casting everything in that pre-storm grayscale that made edges blur. Thunder cracked low and slow, a precursor of what was to come. Mila was already halfway to the lot, moving fast, as if she needed the pending storm to swallow her whole.

Behind us, the diner windows threw rectangles of light across the lot. From certain angles, anyone inside could see out —the glass catching movement more than details. Elise was still in there. So were Avery and Simon. Maybe they would notice, or not. The thought should've stopped me. It didn't.

"Hey." My voice came out rougher than I meant it to.

She didn't stop walking. "What?"

"That guy." I fell into step beside her. "He's not your type."

She stopped then. Turned to face me, eyes narrowed. "Oh, and what is my type, Luke?"

Me. I glared at her. "Not him."

She scoffed. "You don't get to say that. You don't get to look at me that way with her still clinging to you, acting as if she owns you."

"I didn't invite her to sit next to me."

"But you didn't push her away either, did you?"

I wasn't giving her an answer, not when she seemed more than happy to have Simon next to her.

She shook her head. "You think you know me. You don't. Not anymore."

"I know what we are," I said.

Her laugh was soft. Broken. "No. You know what we *were.*"

My fingers itched. And before I could stop myself, I reached out—just a brush of knuckles along the curve of her hip.

She sucked in a breath. Froze. Just stared.

I stepped closer. Her back hit the car behind her. We were in the shadows between two parked cars, mostly hidden from the windows but not invisible. If Elise craned her neck, if Avery looked out at just the right moment… they would see. The risk only made my pulse kick harder.

My hand planted on the metal near her shoulder, caging her in. Her eyes darkened.

"Don't," she whispered.

But when my mouth crashed into hers, it was ignition—a spark to gasoline, and we were already soaked in everything that could burn.

She froze a fraction longer than she should have, like something else was in her head. For a second, I thought she might shove me off. But then her fingers fisted my shirt, gripping me like an anchor, the only thing keeping her from drowning.

And I let her. Because I was already gone.

The way she kissed me—fuck, it was ruin and resurrection. It wasn't soft. It wasn't shy. It was teeth and tongue, a year of silence detonating between us. Every breath we didn't take together. Every word we'd choked back. All of it surged through our bodies, wild as a power line snapping loose.

She tasted of salt and storm and home—every place I'd ever run from and every reason I wanted to stay.

Inside, a burst of laugher hit the glass. Mila broke just long enough to dart a glance toward the diner window, as if half-afraid someone was watching. Her lips were swollen, breath ragged, but when she met my gaze again, she didn't pull away. She kissed me harder, daring the whole damn town to see.

Her mouth moved against mine, as though she could memorize the shape of redemption. Her hands slid up my chest, frantic, trembling, grounding herself and setting fire at the same time.

I grabbed her waist, hauled her tighter against me, her heartbeat crashing into mine. There was no space. No logic. Just her.

She kissed like she'd break if she stopped. As if this was all we had. I could feel her anger in the way she gripped me, taste her fear in the way her breath hitched when I deepened it.

And maybe that was why I couldn't stop. I needed her to feel this. To know I still wanted her. Needed her. That she ruined me and rebuilt me in the same kiss.

I slid a hand in her hair, tilted her chin. She moaned into my mouth, and I swear it undid me.

Because she was right there—broken and bold and mine.

I kissed her, starved, as though she was the only thing that could fill the hollow in my chest. And maybe she was.

She made me desperate. Made me dangerous. And when she pulled away, just barely, breath ragged, eyes wild—I didn't see the girl who left. I saw the girl I never stopped loving. The girl who could still bring me to my knees. Even if she was the one who taught me how to fall.

Then she shoved me back a step, our breath crashing between us. "That can't happen again."

"Why not?" My voice rumbled low.

She blinked up at me. "Because we don't trust each other."

The words hit harder than they should've. I knew why—I'd iced her out the second she came back. She'd vanished without warning, left me with questions and no answers. And she still hadn't told me everything. Not about her mom. Not about that night.

Trust wasn't a switch. It was a thread—frayed, knotted, one pull from snapping.

Then she turned and walked away. This time, I didn't stop her—but not because I didn't want to. Because if I did, I wouldn't let her go again.

CHAPTER TWENTY-THREE

MILA

The studio doors creaked when I pushed them open—same old hinges, same hollow sound echoing off the light wood floor. The building smelled of turpentine and old memories. Today it wrapped around me, a second skin that clung close in familiarity. Comforting. Dangerous.

The lights were half off—motion-sensor sensitive—so the hallway glowed in patches, casting long shadows between each frame lining the wall. I moved through them slowly, fingers grazing the smooth plaster as if touching the space might slow my heartbeat.

From somewhere deeper in the building, muted voices carried—other artists working in another room. But not here. Not in the room with windows that framed the ocean I was most drawn to. The one I'd left behind.

Elise's voice wouldn't leave me. *"I had him before you—and after."* Every time I replayed Luke's kiss, it threaded through. Poisoning the memory. He kissed me like I was the only thing that mattered. But what if it was the same with her too? Was I just another distraction for him?

Thinking that way was what Elise wanted. *Screw her.* I wasn't going to give her the satisfaction. She'd taken up enough space in my head. I was in the studio for a reason, and she did not belong here.

I froze when my gaze settled on a row of oil paintings. Many of them were mine. Shock rooted me in place that they were still there.

They hadn't been moved. Or replaced. Just… there. Tucked among newer ones, older ones. I could pick mine out easily. Rich colors, bold lines, as if I'd bled onto the canvas and didn't know how to stop.

I paused in front of one I'd done of a stormy sea, my fingers tracing the lines I knew by heart, and the past cracked open, rolling through my mind, echoing the thunder outside.

Indigo bled into cerulean, rippling across the canvas, veins frozen beneath ice. I'd swept the brush lower, where a jagged slash of white broke through the darker blues—a foaming crest, violent and alive. I'd added hints of gray, deepening the shadows beneath the waves until the water churned with motion. With each stroke, the sea clawed higher, angry and aching, and still that tiny boat—my boat—tilted into the storm.

It didn't take a genius to know what it meant. That boat was me. Tossed. Isolated. Barely staying afloat.

This was the only place I'd ever felt safe enough to bare everything inside me without fear of it being used as a weapon. Until him.

Here, the past was too close, and because of that, my mind tripped back to a time when warmth wrapped my waist, his chest pressed to my spine. Then scratchy stubble grazed my neck. I jolted a little, a laugh bursting out before I could help it.

"Luke," I said on an exhale, trying to squirm away. "That tickles."

His arms tightened. He nuzzled the hollow beneath my ear, lips brushing over my skin, a quiet promise in the contact. "I thought you liked when I tickled you."

I leaned back into him anyway. "I thought you had a family thing?"

Late afternoon sunlight spilled through the studio's massive windows, painting the floor in gold hues. I stood in front of the easel, facing the wide-open view beyond—the glittering stretch of sand, the skeletal curve of the boardwalk, and just past all that, the ocean I was trying to capture. Feral and endless. Familiar.

"I do," he murmured.

His lips skimmed my neck again, trailing lower. I shivered. My paintbrush clattered to the table beside me, forgotten, landing in a mess of blues and grays and saltwater.

"I did. Don't care. Not going."

I turned my head, just enough to see him in the edge of my vision—windblown hair, cheeks flushed, eyes lit up as though he already knew how dangerous this was. How dangerous *I* was. But he didn't care. That was the problem. Or maybe the miracle.

"Luke—" I started.

He spun me gently until I faced him. His fingers ghosted over my paint-splattered tank top, tracing where the fabric clung to my ribs.

"You looked like you were painting something that was pulling you under." His gaze flicked to the canvas. "So I figured you might need a lifeline."

A breath hitched in my throat. He said things—soft, reckless words—that left bruises in their absence.

I didn't answer. Instead, I rose on my toes and kissed him— quick, salty, paint-scented. Because I couldn't say what I wanted to. Couldn't promise what he needed. Not when I already knew I was the storm.

I blinked back into the present, the past leaving like an old friend slipping through the doorway, and I swallowed hard. The hallway pulsed with silence, broken only by the soft buzz of overhead lights and the echo of his voice in my head. The ache clawed up my spine before I could bury it. We'd almost had everything, until we didn't. And now? There was so much distrust between us, and rightfully so—every step forward wading through quicksand.

I needed space. Movement.

The shared studio was still open, dimly lit but quiet—no one else inside. Thank God.

I crossed to the lockers in the back corner, the ones artists claimed but never really owned. Mine sat third from the end, a streak of dried paint on the edge that could've been anyone's—except I knew it was mine. I'd bled indigo there once. From shaking hands. From not knowing how to stop.

I hesitated, fingers hovering over the lock. The combo came to me before I asked for it. Muscle memory. One right. Two left. One right again. Click. The door creaked open, and air whooshed out of me so fast I had to grip the metal to keep from sinking.

Everything was still here.

Sketchbooks stacked in uneven piles. Half-used tubes of oil paint. A sweatshirt I'd left behind with his last name and hockey number printed on the back. A tin of graphite pencils I hadn't touched since the last time I drew Luke asleep on my couch. Messy. Barefoot. Home.

They hadn't cleared it out. No one had cut the lock or claimed the supplies. I hadn't been erased. I'd been... preserved.

Did he do this? Did Luke make sure they left it untouched?

The idea twisted through me—half agony, half comfort. He was the only one who ever made me feel seen and cared for this way. As though I was more than the hurricane in my blood. Like I could be known and still wanted.

And that was the most dangerous thing of all.

Because this ended. It always ended. When my mom lost control, when her schemes unraveled, when whatever tower she built herself into crumbled—she dragged us with her. And we ran.

She made a game of it when I was little. Pretended we were spies escaping danger, choosing new names, new houses, new lives. But that illusion shattered years ago. Now I just braced for the end of whatever place I managed to carve out.

And this place with Luke? It was never built to survive the blast.

I rested my forehead against the cool metal of the locker, fingers still gripping the edge. I'd promised myself I would never come back here. And yet here I was. Still chasing dreams. Still painting storms. Still wishing for a different ending.

My eyes fell to the pile of tubes stacked in the locker—dried caps, labels smeared with fingerprints I recognized as my own. Graphite tins, familiar brushes, half-crushed rags stiff with old color. Supplies I'd abandoned, still waiting. Still mine.

Before I could think better of it, I scooped up a handful— burnt umber, French ultramarine, titanium white—and carried them to the nearest easel. The sweatshirt with Luke's name still hung over my shoulder, paint-stained and familiar. The smell of turpentine rushed up the second I twisted a cap, thick and sharp, like no time had passed.

The first stroke dragged shaky across the canvas. Then steadier. A sweep of blue, darker at the edges, pulling me under. My hands remembered even if my head didn't want to. Motion took over thought. Shadows. Light. The bones of another storm clawed to life in front of me.

I painted until my breath evened out, until the ache in my chest dulled to something manageable. For a flicker of a second, the canvas didn't look like survival—it looked like possibility. Like I could keep doing this. Make it mine.

The thought scared me more than the truth about my mom. More than Elise. Because wanting a future meant admitting I believed in one.

CHAPTER TWENTY-FOUR

LUKE

The kiss still breathed through me—mind, body, everything. I could taste her. Even after she tore out of the restaurant's parking lot, engine screaming, as if it carried the same ache I did.

I followed behind her. Not close. Just enough to see her veer toward the coast.

The studio.

I took the next turn, forcing my hands to stay on the wheel instead of spinning it back around, pretending I hadn't wanted to chase her down and finish what we started.

It didn't matter.

But it did, because that kiss was burned into my skin—fast and rough and unforgiving. A hit I didn't see coming but had taken straight to the chest. And now? I wanted to go after her.

But Elise's voice echoed in my head: *"Power shifts fast, Luke. You know that."* And there was the message from my mom that the family dinner had been moved to tonight. A weekend night. That didn't happen unless something big was brewing.

And I didn't believe in coincidence.

My phone buzzed. I didn't check it. If it was Mila, I didn't trust myself not to go to her. If it was Elise, I didn't trust myself not to throw the damn phone into traffic.

The King estate sat perched on the north end of town, where the streets turned into private lanes, and the driveways were long enough to land a plane. *Blackwood royalty*, people said. They weren't wrong.

The house came into view—stone and glass and architectural ego. Clean lines. Cold edges. It didn't matter that I'd grown up there. It always made me feel as if I was visiting.

Inside, the house hummed with tension. Claire's laugh drifted from the sitting room, too light to be relaxed. Mom's heels clicked decisively against the hardwood as she entered the dining room with a bottle of red already opened.

"There you are," she said, handing it to the server. "Decant that. He's late."

Not a question. Not a surprise. Just a statement about my father. The man was never early to family dinners. He made a show of walking in last.

Drew stood at the window, his back straight, posture military sharp. His club soda and lime stayed untouched on the credenza. Claire approached him, smoothing the lapel of his jacket lovingly. Her voice was quiet but not private. "You good?"

"Always." Drew's eyes remained on the window.

Bullshit. He only said that when things weren't.

I stepped farther in. Claire looked over at me and smiled—pleasant and too polished, with her stylish dark-blond hair smoothed to perfection and falling just shy of her shoulders. She did her best to look the part of my family but would never fully fit in with the sharks that we were; she was too nice.

"Luke." She moved to kiss my cheek. Her perfume was light and expensive, fitting everything else about her.

"Claire." I nodded but didn't return the smile.

Dinner was served like a board meeting. Everyone took their seats by habit, not invitation. My mom at one end, my dad's empty chair still commanding presence at the other. Drew sat beside Claire. I took the spot across from them, my body taut as it always was at these things.

Mom poured the wine then folded her napkin. "Well. Let's begin."

Dad entered just then, coat draped over his arm, tie loosened —but deliberate. He was power incarnate—gray at the temples, sharp lines carved around his eyes, and a presence that made rooms hold their breath. Mom was his contrast in every visual —blond hair twisted into a perfect French knot, diamonds flashing from ears, throat, fingers. Pale-pink Chanel sleeveless sheath dress that clung to her like a secret she didn't want exposed.

"Apologies," he said. "Lorne needed a few things clarified before our next round of acquisitions."

I didn't miss the look Drew sent him. A flicker of something that might've been approval or irritation or both flashed across his face.

My father sat. "What's so urgent it required rescheduling dinner?"

I leaned forward, fingers laced under the table, deciding to take point on this family get-together. "Elise said something concerning."

My mom set down her fork. "She says a lot of things, dear."

"She implied Dunn Industries is ready to make a move. Something about alliances. Power shifting. She wasn't being subtle."

Drew tilted his head. "She never is. What kind of move?"

"Didn't say. But she offered security. Protection. Suggested when things go sideways for us, she and her father would be a better alliance." I didn't add that it was specifically about me; they could come to their own conclusions there.

My father's expression didn't flicker. But his fingers tapped once against his glass before going still. "Interesting."

My mother's gaze sharpened. "Sounds rehearsed."

"It was," I agreed. "Too clean. Like she'd practiced it."

"She has," Claire added smoothly. "As you know, I'm on good terms with several of the faculty at Blackwood academy. One of the advisors overheard Elise on a call last week. She was asking someone if the PR firm her dad uses could be hired on retainer."

Good terms was one way of putting it. Between donations and discreet favors, half the faculty owed us something. And now I knew how Claire was carving out her place in the game.

"Why would she need PR?" Drew asked.

Claire smiled faintly. "Because she's planning to attach herself publicly to Luke. She wants the optics lined up."

My jaw clenched. I looked at my dad. "What's Dunn Industries doing?"

He considered. "They've been buying up permits. Mostly in the south district. Quiet moves. Nothing flashy. But the volume is… notable."

"Is Lorne involved?" I asked. It seemed if something was going down, he was already in the thick of it. Even though he was a partner, he was more enforcer.

"Not yet," Dad hedged. "But he's aware. And keeping Dunn close."

The door opened then, and Lorne stepped inside as if he'd heard his name. Probably had. The man had a sixth sense for power shifts.

His hair was black with subtle caramel highlights. Tall, with broad shoulders, his presence dwarfed the room in a brutish manner that everyone in his vicinity noted. His custom-tailored suit failed to contain the ruthlessness he wore as a second skin.

He paused at my father's side, whispering something in his ear. My father nodded once.

Lorne moved to Drew next, clapping a hand on his shoulder in passing. The gesture looked casual. But Drew stilled as if someone had pressed pause on his spine.

I watched that touch, memorized it. That was Lorne's version of affection. A hand on your shoulder, heavy enough to mean something, light enough to leave you worrying what. I couldn't help but wonder if that meant Drew had redeemed himself and was moving up in Lorne's eyes in regard to the company.

Lorne stepped back after the shoulder touch and gave a quick nod toward my father. "Just wanted to pass along that information, Grant. I'm off to that client dinner," he addressed to Dad, voice smooth but efficient. "Eleanor. Always good to see you. I'll head out—don't let the first course get cold."

No one laughed, but my mom offered a tight smile.

My dad stood long enough to walk him out. Their voices were low, blurred by the thick walls and heavy doors this house was built for. When he returned, he paused behind his chair, scanning the table, taking stock—of us, of the silence, of whatever came next. Then he sat, smooth and unbothered, as if nothing had shifted at all. Dinner resumed.

Discussion swirled around permits and council votes. My mom asked about a gala. Claire responded with a planned guest list and seating charts. Drew stayed mostly silent, which was never a good sign.

My father caught my eye near the end of the meal. "You're handling Elise?"

"Yes." It was subtle but permission nonetheless to release me from the constraints of his "be nice to Elise" mandate. Not that I was following it anyway. I needed to lock things down with the guys soon—tighten the ranks. Get ahead of whatever storm Dunn was planning to send our way, using his daughter.

His nod was final. "Good."

Mom didn't move on so easily. Her gaze flicked to me, intensity flanked by the glint of her diamond earrings. "Speaking of unexpected returns... I heard Mila Callahan is back in town?"

The entire table shifted. Claire froze, caught mid-motion,

her wine glass suspended mid-air. A muscle twitching near Drew's temple. My father had already warned me about Mila. In the silence, he didn't speak—he just observed, calculating. That was when he was most dangerous.

My mom's voice was deceptively casual. "You were close to that girl before, weren't you?"

I didn't answer right away. That would've given too much away. "I've seen her around," I said finally. "We've talked."

"More than once?" she asked, as though she already knew the answer. As if the question were a test.

"Once or twice." I kept my tone flat.

She nodded, not pleased but not surprised either. "Be careful. Her mother caused… issues, the last time they were in town. That's why she was fired."

Claire didn't look up. Drew's stare was locked on the plate in front of him. My father's fingers tapped once then stopped.

"The problem wasn't just what she did—it was who she did it to. The wrong people remember, Luke. And they don't forget. Stay away from Mila, she'll only bring trouble to our doorstep."

I didn't ask what she meant. Her tone already told me. This wasn't a warning—it was a command. And if I didn't obey, the fallout wouldn't land on just me. It would hit everyone. That was the promise. And if Mila didn't see it yet… she would.

But inside, I wasn't good. Because Mila's kiss was still there. And while the rest of the table talked about threats and positioning and public perception, all I could think about was the girl who tasted of salt and storm and home.

The one I couldn't stay away from. And the one I couldn't afford to chase. Not if I wanted to survive what was coming.

CHAPTER TWENTY-FIVE

MILA

Luke's kiss pulsed under my skin like a second heartbeat—impossible to ignore. I'd tried. I went to the studio along the boardwalk across from the beach to think, to escape. I put my phone across the room. Stared at a blank canvas for twenty minutes. Ignored Avery's texts—three so far, asking if I was coming back out, which I didn't plan to. Because no matter how much I wanted to run into Luke and have it happen again, it couldn't. Too much still hung between us, unresolved.

The rental Mom and I were staying in carried a silence that wrapped around you and whispered all the things you didn't want to hear. Normally, that would've been fine—better, even. But tonight it taunted, as if it knew what I'd done. And what I wanted to do again.

Luke King kissing me was not supposed to happen.

But it did. And now I couldn't stop replaying it. The sound of his breath catching. The way his hands curled into my shirt like he couldn't decide whether to pull me closer or push me away. The heat. The ache. The way the world dropped out from under us and nothing else existed.

My phone lit up again. I glanced at it.

Avery: *Come on, it's just us. You need out of your head. And I promise no more Simon.*

I smiled, a small huff of a breath slipping out. But I didn't answer. Instead, I texted my mom.

Me: *You home tonight?*

I wasn't expecting much. She usually worked late. Or didn't answer. Or gave me a vague timeline that meant nothing. But two minutes later:

Mom: *Just finishing up. Be home in ten. Got stuff for pizza :)*

My chest tightened. She hadn't cooked in weeks. Not real cooking. Not homemade pizza with burnt cheese edges and flour on the floor and music blaring, loud enough to drown out the rest of the world.

When the door opened, she breezed in as if she'd never left. Coat slung over one arm, grocery bag in the other. She looked gorgeous, of course. She always did. A slightly older, more polished version of me—but much prettier. High cheekbones, wide eyes, and a smile that could melt or manipulate depending on her mood.

"Hey, baby," she said, dropping the bag on the counter. "Hope you're hungry. I got everything for pizza. Real pizza. None of that frozen cardboard crap."

I blinked. "You okay?"

She laughed, already pulling her dark hair into a loose bun. "Why? Can't a mom cook dinner without it being a red flag?"

"Not usually."

She shot me a look but grinned. "Fair. Get the flour, will you? Bottom cabinet."

We moved around the kitchen as though we hadn't forgotten how. She tossed me an apron—I caught it midair. I dusted the counter in flour, too much probably, and she shook her head but didn't comment. She found the old cutting board and started chopping vegetables like it was second nature. Somewhere between arguing about pineapple on pizza—absolutely not—and burning the first crust, something in my chest eased.

We danced to an 80s pop playlist. Sang off-key. Laughed too loud. It wasn't perfect, but it was real. And I hadn't had that with her in too long.

After the third mini pizza, she gestured to the living room. "Pick a movie. Something ridiculous. We deserve it."

I picked a rom-com. One with a predictable plot and pretty people pretending heartbreak was something you could solve in ninety minutes. We curled up on the couch, plates balanced on our laps, and for a while, it felt similar to before.

Until it didn't.

I couldn't sit still. My leg bounced. My fingers picked at the crust until the edges crumbled.

Mom paused the movie then turned toward me. "Okay. Spill. You're squirming like you've got ants in your pants."

I hesitated. "It's… about a few things."

Her smile dropped into something quieter. Still soft, but focused.

"The principal," I said. "The one who's giving me the scholarship for the academy. You're still seeing him?"

She nodded. "Until you graduate."

"Is it real?"

She gave a dry laugh. "Real? No. Strategic? Definitely."

I watched her. Tried to read beyond her practiced response. "But is he a good guy?" She said he wasn't dangerous. I wanted to make sure.

"Mila." Her voice dipped, gentler. "Don't waste your empathy on him. He's a mark. He gets to play savior. We get a scholarship and stability. He's not the worst, but don't romanticize it. That's not what this is."

I chewed my lip. "He wants us to move in. Doesn't he?" They always fell hard and fast for her, even if they knew the score.

A flicker of surprise passed through her expression. "He's mentioned it."

"And?"

"And that's not the right angle."

"What is, then?"

She tilted her head, studying me. "You sure you want the answer?"

I nodded once.

"He wants to feel as if he belongs." She broke the crust with her thumb. "Like money and power. But he's not one of them—he's the help. So he clings to me, treating me as his meal ticket into the club. Younger woman, complicated past, pretty enough to distract from the fact that he'll never really sit at the table."

It made my stomach twist. How easily she said it. How transactional it sounded. "And your job? You're working for Elise's dad."

She stilled. "Did something happen?"

"She's a problem. And she's too connected. Are you working directly under him?" If Elise and I came to blows, it wouldn't just be a social fallout—I could cost Mom her job. That was the only reason I hadn't done the damage I'd wanted to.

"Not always. Mostly his second. But he knows who I am."

"Can you find anything out?" I bit my bottom lip, not sure I liked what that said about me, but I was definitely my mother's daughter in ways that mattered—being prepared, forewarned, doing my homework. "About him?"

Her brows lifted. "Why?"

"Because from what Elise is hinting at, he's up to something. And I'm not walking blind through this town anymore."

She leaned back, arms crossed, studying me as if I'd grown another spine. "You're learning."

"I'm surviving. There's a difference." My voice cracked, just slightly. "And I need to know—we're not leaving, right? Not in the middle of the night. No packing bags while it's still dark out. No ditching phones and switching cars. No starting over."

She was quiet for a beat. Then she set her plate on the coffee table and clasped her hands in her lap, all the usual performative ease stripped away. Just her. Just us.

"We're staying," she said, steady and sure. "That's the deal. Until you graduate. I gave you my word, Mila—and I meant it."

Something in my chest unclenched. Not fully. But enough. I nodded. "Okay. Good."

Her hand brushed mine. Brief. Gentle in a way that felt like comfort.

"As for Elise's dad," she went on, voice dropping into something sharper, "he's not clean. Not even close. But the people who deal in shadows don't just hand you their secrets. It takes time. Patience. And access."

"Do you have that?"

"I'm working on it." Her mouth curled, sly. "I always do." She stood, stretching. "Pizza's probably cold."

But I didn't care about the pizza. I just watched her move through the kitchen, part predator, part survivor, part mother— everything I knew and didn't know about her wrapped up in one woman.

I wanted her to say more. That she had a plan. That we would be safe. That all this wasn't just another slow-motion collapse.

But she didn't. She reheated a slice. Sat back down. Pressed play as though none of it weighed her down. And I did the only thing I could. I let her—because Mom was on it. There was a plan in place. And I'd get the information I needed so Elise couldn't ambush me. Or Luke. Not without me seeing it coming first.

CHAPTER TWENTY-SIX

LUKE

The sun was starting to dip when the guys showed up—Chase first, barefoot and already stripping off his shirt, as if nothing about today was different.

Jax brought beer. Theo brought his mouth, which wouldn't stop moving even as he cannonballed into the deep end without warning. I stayed dry. Feet propped on a lounger, making it clear I wasn't planning to move.

No game. No practice. Just the four of us at the pool behind my house. No one else was home. Heat shimmered off the pavement, the water gleaming, smooth as glass under the late-afternoon sun. It was too warm for an autumn day—sticky, heavy with the kind of stillness that warned a storm wasn't far off. The kind of day that made it clear we were on the edge of something.

"Logan's scared shitless." Chase laughed as he passed me a bottle. "Won't even meet my eyes in the hallway."

"Same," Theo added, pushing water off his face and slicking his dirty-blond hair back. "I caught him at lunch. Said he didn't know Mila was gonna be at the bonfire. Swore Elise just told him to make it look good."

"But he watches you, Luke, with hatred burning in his eyes," Jax said.

I took a long drink, letting the cold settle in my chest. I didn't care about his hatred, or even if he tried to start something with me. Bring it. It was Mila who I worried about. "He's not a problem unless he tries something against Mila again." He was Elise's puppet, and that alone made him dangerous to a degree, but since we'd stopped him once, she should change tactics.

"He won't." Jax grinned. "He knows you'll rip his spine out."

"Still." I tipped the bottle toward the pool. "Eyes stay on him."

"Done."

Silence stretched across the patio, thick with unspoken agreement. Not awkward. Not uncertain. Just the kind of quiet that followed decisions already made—no votes needed.

Chase leaned back against the chair, his tone casual. "So what's the move with Elise?"

I didn't flinch. "She thinks I'm still an option."

"And you're not?" he asked.

I kept my face flat. "She's not a threat to me. But she is to the people I don't want touched."

Theo whistled under his breath. "So, what, we ghost her? Blow up her socials? Threaten her boyfriend if she's got one?"

"She doesn't," Jax muttered. "She's been waiting on Luke to get over Mila."

"She'll keep pushing until she's slapped down," I muttered. "We just need to decide how clean we want it."

Jax shifted in his seat. "You want her scared? Or exposed?"

"Both," I admitted. "But no drama. No sloppiness. We do this wrong, her dad gets involved." And Charles Dunn wasn't someone we wanted to deal with, not yet anyway.

And that was a bigger problem. Because Dunn didn't just pull strings—he rewired the whole damn game board. Power wasn't enough for him. Control was. Every woman in his orbit was a pawn—Elise included. He treated them as accessories to his image. Replaceable. Silenced. Useful only so long as they bent to his agenda. The man was a textbook misogynist, the kind who wore tailored suits and smiled for cameras while gutting people from the inside out.

"That's happening," Chase said. "If Mila's mom is under Dunn, then it's already crossed into family lines."

I nodded once, gaze fixed past the pool, past the house, past everything. "Which means Elise won't stop. This'll piss her off, make her reckless. But she's not broken. Not yet." Not enough to leave Mila alone.

"Good," Jax muttered. "Means we'll see her coming."

I wasn't so sure. Elise didn't need to attack head-on. She'd smile while she cut you.

I nodded once. "Which is why we can't touch Elise physically. No threats. We cut her out socially. Cold. Let her feel the sting of being invisible."

Theo frowned. "She'll come harder."

"Let her." I leaned forward, elbows on my knees. "That's when we corner her. When she's desperate."

"And Logan?" Chase asked. "We letting him walk?"

I thought about it. About his smirk. His retreat. His shitty little shrug as though he wasn't part of it.

"Not yet," I said. "But if he so much as breathes wrong near Mila—"

"I'll deal with it," Jax cut in, jaw clenched. "He's overdue for a reminder."

Chase snorted. "You always think someone is."

"But this one's personal," Jax said. "He doesn't get to scare girls. Not without consequence."

We all knew the reason, but none of us voiced it—Avery was too close to Mila, and the fallout could affect her. "Good. But nothing that lands us in the office. We're ghosts until it counts."

"Copy that."

Theo dragged a towel over his head and tossed it aside. "So what about Mila?"

"She's not involved," I snapped, sharper than I meant it.

"She kissed you back," Jax reminded me.

I stared out at the water. I'd told them, or I had when they'd guessed. "Doesn't matter. Her mom's tied to Dunn. That's too close." *For now.* "I don't keep anyone close if there's a chance they're working both sides."

"You think Elise knows?" Chase asked.

"She suspects." I looked at him. "About Mila and what she means to me." That was the game now—see how far she could push before I snapped.

Theo extended his legs. "And you? You're good with walking away from Mila?"

I didn't answer, just let the quiet speak for me. They didn't push. They knew what silence meant in our group. Mila was a weak spot. They didn't need the details to know the truth.

"I'll protect her if it comes to that." I met their gazes with a promise in my own. "But anything more? It ends with that kiss."

"Hard lines," Jax said. "I like it."

"Hard lines keep us alive," I reiterated. "And untouchable."

The sun dipped lower, casting long shadows across the pool deck. I watched them stretch like cracks in the concrete.

None of us moved. Not yet.

We'd made a plan. Started the freeze by messaging a few select people—the kind who would spread the word fast. Now we just had to wait—because Elise wouldn't go quietly. And when she struck back, that was when the real trap would spring.

CHAPTER TWENTY-SEVEN

MILA

There wasn't enough coffee in the universe to prepare me for a Monday at Blackwood Academy. But here I was, making the best of it. Speaking of the best of it, I needed to find Avery. I passed through the ornate wooden double doors of the entryway into academic hell then made my way through the corridor toward my locker, where I hoped I would find her.

The hallway felt lighter, charged with something I couldn't claim. It was the oddest sensation. I studied faces as I went forward, noting that few observed me and instead, everyone was looking at whoever must've been behind me. I fought from turning. It wasn't Luke or any of those guys. I would've seen an array of expressions from desperation to wanton lust painted across the female population, but that wasn't what I saw.

When a ripple moved through the crowd, followed by quick glances over shoulders, heads subtly turning, I fell prey to curiosity and followed their gazes until mine found Elise.

She entered the same way she always did—spine rigid, flanked by Nina and Tori, decked head to toe in designer clothes, hair perfectly styled, and makeup on point. But this time, the current around them didn't pull people in. It pushed them back.

A group near the vending machines scattered without a word. Two girls who normally smiled hopefully at Elise as she passed stared at their phones instead, mouths twitching with what looked suspiciously like *smirks*. A guy from the soccer team brushed by without so much as a nod.

The orbit had shifted. Elise still walked as if she owned the place. But today, no one bowed. And I was so there for it.

She stopped at the center of a group of football players who normally fell at her feet salivating. Today, they parted like water, silent. One of them glanced at her, then at me, and turned away mid-smirk. Another crossed his arms. No greeting. No sly invitation. Just cold entry, closed off.

The smallest hitch in her step. Barely there. But I saw it.

Other people noticed. Girls who usually hovered near Elise gave each other looks of disbelief—some smirked; some whispered. The higher echelon who aspired to gain entry into her inner circle, who were just underneath her sphere of power, seemed to shrink a little, unsure. Even the junior clique, free of her reach before, straightened. Bold. Because Blackwood's reigning queen somehow just got shoved off her throne—and everyone, except me, was aware of it.

I caught Avery's eye near my locker as I joined her for the show that was unfolding before us.

She raised a brow and whispered, "Did she just get iced out?"

Before I could respond, I saw it: Elise's face tightened, scanning the crowd for weakness. Her mouth moved, like she was about to say something to Nina, but nothing came out. She stalked toward the east wing lockers, where Luke, Jax, Chase, and Theo stood as sentries. They stood with arms crossed or thumbs hooked in pockets, backs to the lockers—owning the hallway as if it had always belonged to them.

She slowed as she approached, smile clipped in place. More

teeth than warmth. More defiance than charm. But no one moved to greet her.

Luke didn't look at her, but he said something, and her head snapped back as if slapped. His arms were crossed, back resting against the lockers like the conversation he resumed with the guys couldn't be interrupted. Jax angled his body, cutting her off with his shoulder. Chase ran a hand through his hair and turned deliberately toward Theo, laughing, ignoring Elise completely, effectively shielding her from their group.

She tried to step in, to close the distance—but the four of them held formation. No shift. No crack. Like the group was sealed.

Theo's eyes flicked to Tori, quick and unreadable. She hesitated at Elise's flank, chin tilted like she wanted to say something—but Theo's expression didn't change. Neutral. Cold. Not hostile. Just… done.

Elise stood there, frozen in that space where power used to part the waters—and this time, it didn't. No one shifted to make room. No one stepped aside. Her jaw twitched. Shoulders rose, then locked. The moment stretched too long. Then she turned, heels clacking against the wood floor, each step a punishment as she stormed away.

I watched the space she left behind. The void. The silence. Then I glanced toward the group that used to flock around her like satellites. "Yeah," I finally responded to Avery. "She's being shut out."

Avery exhaled—slow, satisfied. "About time."

But she didn't whisper it. And Elise wasn't out of range. The sound of heels stopped. Elise turned on a dime, fury painting her cheeks red. Her eyes flashed retribution as they settled on Avery, narrowing. "Jealousy doesn't suit you." Her voice dripped venom. "Then again, neither does cheap lip gloss or pretending you matter."

Avery blinked. "Better cheap than expired." Her smile was dagger-sweet.

Elise's lips twitched. Her icy gaze dropped briefly to Avery's linked arm with mine then slid back up. "Watch who you stand next to. You'll get dragged down along with dead weight." Then she turned again—except her walk was stiffer now, clipped, a clock running out of seconds.

Girls scattered in her path, but this time it wasn't reverent—it was reactive. As though stepping aside to avoid the fallout.

Around us, the hall hummed. Whispers uncoiled down the row: *"Did you see that? Was she just iced out?"* One girl nudged her friend, pointing without subtlety at Elise's retreating form. Another laughed too loudly as she passed.

The tiers were shifting. And the top just got lighter.

I let go of Avery's arm and got to work opening my locker, the combination muscle memory. The lock clicked, metal clanged. I grabbed what I needed without looking.

Around us, every step and every sound felt charged—low and electric—a storm humming beneath the floor. I'd just closed my locker when a familiar presence shifted in behind Avery's.

Jax. He leaned casually, back against the metal as if he'd been there the whole time. But his eyes weren't on me. Or Avery. They were trained on Elise's retreating form.

Elise glanced over her shoulder—just once—and caught sight of Jax next to Avery. Her expression hardened, turning even more determined as her focus slid to me. It was that vindictive look she gave right before she would say something cruel in passing that would fester for days. Except this time, she didn't say a word as her eyes flicked back to the hulking guy beside us. Her red lips compressed into a tight line.

He didn't speak, didn't posture, just squared his broad shoulders. Subtle. Deliberate. A line drawn in silence.

She hesitated. Blinked once. Then walked faster.

He pushed off the locker, half-smirking, voice low. "She can't touch you, Aves. If she tries, I'm your enforcer."

Avery's cheeks turned faintly pink. "Thanks, Jax."

He didn't answer. But he gave her a slow once-over, as if he was checking that she was okay, then glanced at me. Nodded once before walking off, as though he hadn't just made a statement loud enough for the hallway to hear—and for her brother to note.

I bit back a smile. Because the fall of a queen didn't always come with a scream. Sometimes, it came with silence—and a guy choosing who he stood beside. Avery's grin cracked wide. Relief, satisfaction, and maybe a flicker of something else.

I felt that flutter too. A secret smile tugged at my mouth. Jax had finally made a move. Even if it was small.

Avery elbowed me, whispering, "Did he seriously just do that? With my brother ten feet away?"

I watched Jax pass Chase without a word. "Bold move."

A few girls drifted by, curiosity outweighing caution. Nods. Half-smiles. Quick, whispered shorthand passed between them —"You saw that. She's not untouchable anymore."

The morning passed in a blur, and suddenly it was lunch. The cafeteria was loud. The rumor mill buzzed. Elise sat at her usual table, alone this time except for Nina and Tori flanking her, but they didn't speak. They didn't laugh. The glow around them had dulled, except when Elise snapped at anyone nearby who dared to say anything—tight voice, flaring nostrils, commanding the whispers that barely reached past the rim of her table.

People were getting bold—maybe too bold. I didn't trust that her power was completely gone. Elise was a snake. She didn't need a crown to strike.

As the clock ticked down, I took note—who cheered too loud at her fall, and who, the ones seasoned in survival, kept their heads down and eyes sharp.

Later, as Avery and I sat with a cluster of second tiers and outliers, Elise passed. Her gaze swept the group, landing on me sharp as a blade. No one flinched, and I didn't look away. Didn't blink.

That was enough.

As we left the cafeteria, Avery spun to face me, voice low. "She'll come back swinging. She always does."

I nodded. "Let her."

She hesitated. "Are you... glad? About her getting knocked down?"

I glanced at her. "I don't care if she's queen of this place or a cautionary tale. Long as she doesn't touch us." I adjusted my backpack strap. "If she does, someone'll finish what got started today."

Avery let out a short, delighted exhale and thumped the wall with her fist. I laughed—real, full, the kind that scraped something loose inside me.

Out of instinct, I glanced toward the lockers again. Toward him.

But as we moved toward class, I clocked it—not once had Luke looked at me during lunch. Not even a glance. Not when I walked in. Not when the room shifted around Elise.

We weren't anything. But the kiss we shared sure as hell said otherwise, even if he wasn't going to admit it. And yeah—it stung. Just a flicker, enough to feel.

I needed to stop thinking about it. About how his hand gripped my hip. About how I wanted to kiss him again. And it looked as though we weren't going to. That was fine—sort of— as there were other things that needed to take precedence.

Because I couldn't shake the feeling that Elise wasn't finished. Her warning stuck like a sliver beneath skin. I reached for calm, for control. For intel. Had my mom found anything I could use if Elise came again? And if she had... would I share it with Luke in an attempt to heal the wrong I'd done him when I'd left before or keep it for when I needed it most?

CHAPTER TWENTY-EIGHT

LUKE

The ice rink felt alive under the bright lights—electric, vibrant energy pulsing through the boards as we skated out for warm-ups. Fans hollered, bodies pressing against plexiglass, but I ignored them. My eyes tracked Mila in the stands—Avery sat next to her and her two other friends on either side.

Jax passed the plexiglass separating them from the ice and tapped it with his stick. Avery jumped. Jax smirked. Chase's jaw clenched so tight a muscle pulsed near his ear. I nodded at him—keep it together. That was the message.

No personal shit tonight. We had a game to win.

By the time line changes were called, we were up by one.

Theo had slipped it past the goalie after I'd drawn the defense and threaded the puck clean through the gap. Textbook setup. Easy finish. The kind of play that reminded everyone exactly why we were ranked where we were.

The team we were up against didn't rate—on paper or on ice, forecasting a clean win. But the real game wasn't happening on the scoreboard. As I stepped off the ice to our bench, I zeroed in on Logan.

Third line, he sat hunched at the edge of the bench, waiting for his chance. When he finally got the call to take the ice, his stride was tight, caged frustration. He barely touched the puck, his play sloppy enough that Coach noticed.

A line change was called, and he skated back. On the bench, he muttered with a linemate, stiff-shouldered. But he kept glancing my way.

Chase muttered behind his mouthguard, "That wasn't nerves. He's plotting something."

Jax leaned forward slightly, tracking Logan's retreat to the bench. "Yeah. Eyes like that? He's not done. Just waiting for the right time to strike."

I didn't respond, keeping my focus forward. Because I'd seen it too. And whatever Logan was plotting—it wasn't over. I kept my expression unreadable.

Logan's linemate caught the exchange and said something low as they hit the bench. Logan muttered back, stiff-shouldered, and didn't look up again. Because he knew. Just from that one slipup, we'd taken note, and we weren't done with him yet.

The Zamboni took to the ice. I stayed back while the rest of the team filed toward the locker room. I needed a second to breathe.

That was when I saw Drew, slipping into a seat just behind the glass—one row up from where Mila and Avery sat. He didn't wave. Didn't nod. Just leaned forward, tie loose, suit jacket folded over one arm, and eyes intense beneath the press of arena lights. I caught his gaze. Focused. Steady. A silent signal that I wasn't carrying this weight alone.

But it wasn't Drew I kept glancing back to.

Mila sat forward as she had most of the time we were on the ice, elbows on her knees, eyes narrowed—not on the game but something distant. Distracted.

What happened? The question burned hotter than it should've. The look on her face made me want to defy my family's mandate and take the weight from her shoulders.

Drew moved to intercept me on the way to the locker room. I let my teammates bypass us while I stepped to the side. Drew didn't normally come to my games. Something had to be up.

We both remained silent until the last of my teammates filed into the locker room, Logan being among the stragglers. When I glanced at my brother, I clocked him watching Logan as the door shut after him. Drew caught my gaze, noting that I'd seen where he was looking.

"I heard something and wanted to give you a heads up, keep you in the know." He notched his head in Logan's direction. "Logan Mitchel's dad lost everything—fired, stripped of his pension, drowning in dept." Drew's voice was low, rough. "Last I heard, his father's not doing well. Drinking, behind on mortgage, car payments, probably even his kid's tuition. Watch out for the kid, bet he's holding a grudge."

Drew's mouth flattened. "And it doesn't end there. I caught wind that Dunn's people are circling—dangling favors, promises. Dunn knows a vendetta when he sees one, and he's not above weaponizing it. So, if Logan looks like he's just a jealous prick over Elise? Don't buy it. There's more at play."

Sweat rolled down my face. Cold dread twisted behind my ribs.

Drew continued. "Logan's a loose cannon. Same as his old man when it comes to anyone with the last name King."

"Noted." He'd told me enough to sketch out Logan's play. This wasn't about chasing Elise—it was about securing a future, claiming a business heiress to rebuild from the ashes of what his family lost. To make the people responsible pay.

"You need to stay ten steps ahead. Don't get blindsided."

I snapped back into the conversation. "I won't."

Coach stuck his head out and yelled for me to get my ass into the locker room. I nodded but paused when Drew grasped my bicep.

"Luke—whatever's happening with Mila? Don't let it blur the lines."

"I don't plan on it," I ground out, irritated that he'd noticed. That anyone had. He gave a single nod, but his eyes lingered—as though he knew more than he was saying, or he was waiting for me to prove him wrong.

"Good."

I jerked a nod and stalked off toward the locker room. I didn't need a reminder. Especially not from Drew. I knew exactly what was expected of me. What this family demanded. But that didn't stop the anger from climbing up my spine.

As I slapped my palms against the locker room doors and shoved them open, Logan's name kept circling in my mind. His father. Dunn. Mila. Elise. Drew's warning rang louder than the cheers rumbling through the arena walls when we'd scored earlier. The pieces were stacking, and none of them felt random.

Coach did his thing. I was there, but not. Thinking, waiting to get back on the ice. By the time we were cleared to leave the locker room, I was salivating for the game. Needing the hit of adrenaline, the clean rush of focus. Anything to shut my brain off.

The second we hit the ice again, instinct kicked in, and we dominated. I blocked a shot that should've slipped through the crease. Theo scored one more off a feed I barely remembered sending. I shot two into the corner of the net. By the final buzzer, fans were on their feet, the rink vibrating with noise. We didn't celebrate hard—this wasn't the kind of win we let go to our heads. It was too easy. And my mind was focused on different battles.

In the locker room, the mood stayed level. Not tense, not loose. Focused.

Chase peeled off his pads. "Logan didn't make a move toward Mila or Aves when he filed past them."

"Yet," Jax added, towel slung over his neck.

"He will." I untied my skates. "His dad got fired from King Enterprises—lost the pension, lost the stability. Now Logan's circling like he's got something to prove."

"Against you? Us?" Chase asked.

I nodded once. "He's desperate. And desperation makes people reckless."

Theo leaned back on the bench, stretching his shoulder. "So what's his play? Is he trying to tie himself to Elise and score something for his dad—or is it personal?"

"Could be both," I said. "Elise's dad's no joke. That family could open doors. Or hand him a loaded gun."

Jax cracked his knuckles. "The guy's been one bad day from snapping since we got here."

"And Elise?" Chase asked.

"The freeze is holding," I said. "So far. Regardless, we don't let our guard down. Not with her."

Theo grinned, shaking water into his hair from a water bottle. "I'll keep her friend busy. Tori talks post-hookup."

The room rumbled with their low laughter.

"Taking one for the team?" Jax smirked.

"I'm committed to the mission," Theo said, mock-serious.

"Yeah, committed to what's between her legs," Chase muttered.

I let them joke. It was good for morale. But under it, we all knew the game had changed.

I stood, yanking my shirt over my head. "Watch Elise, watch Logan. We control the story. Not the other way around."

The silence that followed wasn't empty as they nodded their agreement. It was loaded. Lines were drawn.

CHAPTER TWENTY-NINE

MILA

I couldn't keep my mind on the game. Luke and the other guys blurred across the ice while my thoughts tunneled back to what Mom told me before I left the house.

She had been waiting for me when I got home. Unusual for her to be around that early, even stranger the way she sat—purse perched on her lap, hair still twisted tight, as if she'd barely paused. There had been a gleam in her eye. Not pride. Not exactly triumph. Banked intensity.

"I went digging." Her lips curved at the corners. "You asked me to look into Dunn. I did."

I didn't breathe.

"They're buying up King Enterprises stock and real estate—quiet moves through companies. The trail's clean if you don't know where to look. I do."

I stared at her. "Why?"

Her mouth curled—not quite a smile. "Because you asked."

I could barely find my voice. "Will you get caught?"

She shook her head no then glanced at her phone before standing. "I took a late lunch to tell you. I've got to head back to the office. Now you know. And, Mila,"—she waited until our gazes locked—"be careful with this information. These are heavy hitters. They don't play fair or nicely."

And just that quickly, she was gone again. Back to her job. Back to Dunn. The principal. Back to pretending.

But I wasn't pretending. Not anymore.

So here I was at the rink, because Avery had dragged me out that evening. Throughout the game, I couldn't follow anything. They'd scored? I went along and pretended to know what was going on by mimicking Avery. I needed more than a moment to weigh whether to tell Luke what I'd learned or keep it buried. Because it meant something huge for his family business, his legacy.

The information gnawed at me. After the final buzzer, we gathered by the exit, and I'd made my decision. Avery and I waited by her blue Mercedes. Her two friends—Jasmine and Margie—floated nearby, flirting with two guys from our school.

Chase clocked them and barked, "Aves!" He bounded over, the rest trailing.

Avery lurched toward him, throwing her arms around her brother in a congratulatory hug. As she pulled away, Jax leaned in just enough to murmur something that made her roll her eyes, but she didn't move away. Her smile tugged at the corner, as though she refused to give him the satisfaction.

I stood back, unsure. I mumbled something vague—"Great game, congrats"—then edged away as Jasmine and Margie joined her. Luke's hooded gaze followed with banked intensity, as if he was trying to read me.

I leaned into the small gap between me and the trunk, edging away from everyone else as much as I could without notice.

"Luke…" I kept my voice low. The last thing I wanted was to light a match that could ignite into wildfire—especially when his family might still have a chance to quietly control the fallout.

He shifted my way, closing the space between us, that damn muscle ticking in his jaw.

"I found out about something that you need to know."

He didn't speak, just waited for me to continue.

"My mom... she told me Dunn Industries is buying King Enterprises stock and properties through shell companies."

Luke's jaw shifted. His eyes darkened. There was something unreadable building behind them. A warning. Or maybe accusation. It hit like a door shutting quietly in my face.

He exhaled slow enough I felt it move between us.

"My mom works for Dunn," I added for full disclosure.

He didn't respond.

"I wanted to tell you, give you fair warning about what I'd learned. This time is different." My voice barely carried, the weight of it settling like a brick wall between us. He knew what I'd meant—I wasn't running. I was standing my ground, fighting alongside him. It wasn't like before, even though he had no idea why I'd had to leave in the first place. I was choosing to let him in. To trust him with what I knew. To fight instead of run.

"Your mom works for Dunn."

I blinked. "Yeah, I told you—"

"It makes your intel suspect." His voice was cold, hard, flat. "You don't think Dunn would feed her misinformation? Use you as a pawn?"

The chill emanating from him cracked something in me. "That's where we're at?" My breath caught, betrayal slicing through me. "You think I'm being used? Or you think I'm working against you." That last one wasn't a question. The wall that fell over him told me my answer.

Luke's jaw flexed, eyes fixed somewhere past me, as if I wasn't even worth the direct hit. "You think I can ignore what my brother told me? What my family's already laid out? Your mom stole from us. Now she works for Dunn. You walk back into my life like nothing's changed, and I'm supposed to forget where your loyalty lies?"

My stomach dropped. "You think I would sell you out? After everything?"

His gaze finally cut to mine, flint and fury. "I think you don't even have to try. All Dunn has to do is pull strings, and your family dances. You can claim you don't know, you can say you're not part of it—but you carry their shadow. And I can't let that near me again."

The words hit harder than his silence ever could have. It wasn't just distrust—it was exile. And it burned like betrayal.

"You wouldn't trust anything that I tell you, would you?"

"I trust patterns," he said.

I let out a hollow laugh that scraped my throat raw. "Patterns. That's all I am to you now? A tally of every way I've already let you down? You don't even see me—you see what you're afraid of. And you've already decided I'm guilty."

His expression didn't change. "Right. Because a girl who fucked me over in the past knows how this ends."

His rejection hit with the force of a riptide. My throat burned, my head spun, lungs clawing for air. "That kiss…" I shook my head, barely breathing. "Guess it didn't mean a damn thing to you." Because to me? It meant everything. Which only proved how stupid I'd been to let him anywhere near my heart again.

He stepped back, eyes hard. "Maybe it meant we were both stupid. Just for different reasons."

He turned—no hesitation, no apology—and walked straight into the crowd, as if I hadn't just handed him a piece of me I never should have given him. Like it was easy. As if I was disposable. Forgettable.

I replayed his words on a loop, each one slicing deeper. *"All Dunn has to do is pull strings, and your family dances."*

He didn't see me—he saw them. My mom's paycheck. Her

boss's shadow. Every choice I made tangled in someone else's agenda, as though even my breath belonged to Dunn's plan.

It wasn't just that he didn't trust me. It was worse. He trusted Drew more. He trusted his family's rules more. He trusted what had already happened more than me.

And that? That was betrayal. Because whatever else I'd done, I would never choose Dunn over him. Why would I? Because my mom worked for them? Because we needed the money and that was her only option? But Luke—he had just chosen the Kings over me.

My chest ached, splintered clean through. I wanted to scream, to hit something, to kiss him until he remembered—but all I could do was swallow it down and keep standing. Because breaking in front of him would've been the same as proving him right.

Avery approached from the side. "You good?"

I nodded once, stiffly. "Fine. Just ready to go."

She didn't press, just shot a glare at Luke's retreating form before sliding into the driver's seat. I followed, hands trembling as I opened the passenger door. Her friends climbed into the back, thankfully too caught up in their own chatter to notice my world had just come undone.

As Avery pulled away, I couldn't stop myself from looking— one last glance out the window. He didn't turn. Didn't try to stop me. It was over. Truly over, before anything real had even begun.

Fuck him. I took a page from his playbook—and didn't look back either.

CHAPTER THIRTY

LUKE

The parking lot had thinned out. Mila and Avery tore out of there after what I'd said. The guys took one look at me and didn't ask why I was leaving.

Once I got behind the steering wheel, I took off, leaving everything behind me.

My jaw was tight, stomach burning. I needed to smash my fist into something. A bag. A wall. The dashboard. The look on Mila's face haunted me—shocked, shattered—after I shut her out when all she'd done was be honest. Because that was what had happened there. Even if her information was tainted, a lie, she was innocent. She'd tried to bring it to my attention—to protect me.

Drew's words from earlier circled back, digging under my skin. *"...whatever's happening with Mila? Don't let it blur the lines."* I'd told him she wouldn't. I believed it. But right now, those lines were smudged and fading.

She never hid what she wanted most—made no secret of her dreams, or how badly she believed in things most people gave up on. Me included. And I could always tell when she was holding back or hiding something. This wasn't one of those times.

But when it came to her reality, the hard parts with her mom, with moving? She stayed locked up. And I let her. Back then, I didn't push. Figured if she wanted to talk, she would. She didn't. Not about the ugly things she'd experienced.

And tonight, she'd finally tried. I'd held the rules tighter than any affection, because the mandate was clear: *Stay away.*

She'd tried to open up to me—and I drowned it with cold logic and distance. Shut her out, as though she hadn't just handed me the kind of truth most people hoard. And now she was gone. She'd been sitting next to Avery, eyes fixed on the road, as if none of it touched her. But I knew better. She didn't fall apart. She pulled back. And for a moment, what gutted me wasn't that I'd pushed her away and she'd let me. It was how much I wanted her, and the thought that she might not look back. That she might never let me in again.

I pushed away the ache and drove home the only way I knew —fast. Brakes kissed skid marks into the driveway when I arrived home. I killed the engine, sat there for half a second, then shut the door hard enough to echo.

The front windows glowed, shadows moving behind the glass—Mom, probably on a call. Dad, probably still at the office. Drew, maybe upstairs. I didn't care to find out. I slipped through the side entrance, bypassed the kitchen, and took the back hall straight down to the gym.

There was too much noise in my head. I yanked the door to the fully stocked workout room wide, kicked it shut behind me, stripped off my shirt, and then grabbed the heaviest dumbbells I had. I dropped them onto the mat, as if punishing steel could take what I couldn't say. Then I started lifting—fast, hard, punishing. Swing. Press. Slam. Rep. Again. Sweat burned down my spine, muscles shrieking with every move.

I needed it to hurt. Needed something to crack. If I couldn't rip her out of my head, maybe I could outrun the guilt grinding behind my ribs.

That was when Drew slipped in. I caught his reflection first, a flicker in the mirror. It took everything in me to corral my emotions before giving him my attention. He didn't speak. Just leaned against the squat rack—arms crossed, a crooked curve to his lips—one of the things that reminded me we were brothers. We had the same crooked grin, the same eyes. But not much else lined up. I had three inches on him, the athlete's frame. He was stockier. Bulldog.

"What's going on?" He waved a hand to encompass all of me. "Looks like you're working through a problem. Did Logan start something?"

I dropped the dumbbells, hitting the water bottle, which sloshed across the mat. "No. I found something else out. Not sure if it's true, considering the source."

"The source?" Drew moved closer, voice quiet, danger shadowing his frame.

I hesitated. The need to protect Mila was undeniable. "Doesn't matter, what does is the information." I told him what she'd relayed to me about Dunn—the shell companies, the stocks, and the real estate.

Fury crackled through Drew's eyes before it solidified into determination. "It fits. I'll bring this to Dad's attention." He gripped my shoulder before releasing it. "This is good. That's what a future partner does—keeps the company protected. With this, we won't be in reaction mode. We don't wait. We go preemptive and offensive now. That gives us leverage. And when I share this with Dad—he'll see. You did good."

My brother meant well. He was trying to give me credit. Make me look strong. Strategic. Loyal. But none of that mattered. Not when the only thing I could see was Mila's face when I shut her down.

I left the weight room without a word, my steps heavy. I

avoided the main hall, slipping out the side door, as if I had something to hide—because I did.

The sky had gone dark, the kind of black that hummed with questions you didn't want to answer. I got into my SUV and sat there for a beat, gripping the wheel until my knuckles turned white. Then I drove with no plan or direction—just momentum and regret. Because she'd offered me something real—and I'd crushed it before I even realized what I was holding.

CHAPTER THIRTY-ONE

MILA

After Avery dropped me off at home, I got in my car and drove straight to the studio on the boardwalk. The sun painted a rippling path of red, orange, and gold across the water's surface. I barely registered it. Didn't care. My mind had been locked down since Luke's rejection.

It was after hours. I punched in the code Luke had given me when I'd lived here before for the side door's keypad. His family owned the building, but it was rented to a community art collective.

The lock clicked open, and I hesitated. *He never changed it.* My mouth pulled down, and I shook my head. It was oversight, not symbolism. I couldn't let it mean more.

Once inside, I flipped the switch and made my way to the paint studio—the one place I could bleed without making a sound. My fingers brushed across the canvas of my old oil painting. Ocean waves. A small boat in the middle of nowhere. Crisis captured in pigment and grief. Fitting. Once again, I was that boat.

I moved to the back room where my supplies were kept. After working the lock on my cabinet, I pulled out a sketchbook and graphite pencils. Color didn't suit me right now. The world was gray, stripped, raw. Graphite matched the mood.

Disgust crawled over my skin, phantom fingers dragging across me. Even I was getting tired of the drama looping in my chest.

My hand hovered over the metal spiral before flipping the cover open to a page where I'd sketched him—eyes shadowed, mouth tight, something raw barely caged behind the lines of his face. Not cold. But guarded, struggling. The sketch captured what I'd seen in him that night—the fight to hold it all together.

My throat burned. I tore the page out, crumpled it in one tight fist, and threw it toward the trash. I didn't check where it landed. Didn't need to.

Restless, I wandered the studio halls. My paintings, mixed among other artists, watched in silence. Their textures shadowed in the low light, but they were still here. Still mine. Some part of me—sacred and stubborn—refused to be erased.

I'd run most of my life—because of situations Mom and I found ourselves in. It was survival. Instinct. Since I was a kid, I was always leaving behind towns, schools, people, hope. But this time? I wanted to stay. Even if it was hard. Especially when it hurt. Stranded in the echo of what I'd lost. And maybe... what I'd almost had.

I drifted to the boardwalk window. Outside, the ocean blinked with scattered lights, waves swallowing the shore in slow motion. I let it all settle—my chest, my limbs, my thoughts. Let the quiet take over.

And somewhere in that stillness, a promise solidified—*never again will I hand someone a piece of me without knowing they'll hold on to it.*

An hour later and back home, I lay face-down on my bed, eyes red-rimmed, throat raw. My shirt twisted to one side, the blanket tangled around me—a trap I didn't have the energy to escape.

A soft knock tapped the door. Then it creaked open. "Mila, are you all right?" Concern punctured Mom's softly spoken question.

I didn't answer.

She crossed the room and sat beside me, tugging the blanket back, her fingers smoothing down my hair. "Did Elise do something? Is that what's wrong?"

I blinked. "What?" My voice cracked. "No. Why would I care about her?"

"You asked me for information on Dunn. I thought you were trying to get leverage against her."

Her words drifted, not quite connecting. I forced myself to sit up, swiping my hands over my still wet cheeks. "No. It's not about Elise."

She studied me, a slow dawning horror settling behind her eyes. "Is this about Luke King?"

The silence that followed was answer enough.

"Oh, Mila." She stood up too fast and paced, ripping the elastic band from her hair. "I never thought you'd let him back in. Not again."

My heart thudded. "What are you talking about?" I shifted on the bed, dropping my legs over the edge. "What are you keeping from me?"

She didn't respond, and determination solidified inside me to push for answers. "Mom? Why are we really back here? And not the reasons you've already given me. I want the real one, the root cause of us returning to Blackwood."

Her lips pressed together as she looked at me over her shoulder before pivoting and retracing her steps back to the side of my bed.

"Mom, why does it feel like we walked back into a minefield?"

More silence, but at least she'd stilled. Then, carefully, "Because we are."

I froze. The air in my bedroom thickened, as if it knew what was coming before I did. "Say that again."

"I didn't want to bring you back. Not this way. But they found me. Said they had a job—clean up some books, make a few irregularities disappear. Big money, quick timeline, no paper trail. And before I could say no, they said your name."

My chest tightened. "Who?"

"They didn't give names."

"You said we ran because of the boyfriend," I whispered. "Because of the murder."

"We did. But that was the match. Not the gasoline."

I stood, bracing myself against the headboard, knuckles pale. "Tell me what you saw."

Another beat of silence. Then, slowly, "That night, I went back to the office at King Enterprises after a company-wide email was sent out saying Darren had taken a job overseas, and anything he had been working on would be filtered through Stephanie until they had a replacement for him. I had a bad feeling. Especially since it was the first I'd heard of him leaving, and immediately too. My instincts screamed something was wrong. I logged in to pull the files I'd been keeping—proof that funds were being diverted into shell companies tied to people I was told never to mention. But the accounts were scrubbed. Clean. As if I'd never touched them." She paused, as if the memory still clawed at her. "Our names were gone, Mila. Yours too. From school records, emergency contacts, even your medical files. They were erasing us."

"Why?"

"Because someone needed a loose end tied off. Darren got curious. Started poking around where he shouldn't. He told me he'd found something—said he would make it right. Two days later, he was dead." Her voice faltered, dropping lower. "And before you got there... I saw Lorne. He was standing over Darren's body. Gun in hand." A shaky inhale. "He didn't see me.

But the way he stood there... steady. Calm. As though nothing about it was unusual or surprising. I was frozen. Then you got there."

A tremor raced through me. Cold. Too cold. The kind of stillness that meant he'd already decided what came next. This was beyond bad.

"That's why we ran," she said. "I thought we could disappear before they decided we were next."

My chest caved in. *Lorne.* The untouchable partner in King Enterprises. The Kings were at the root of everything we'd run from.

But Luke was different. I still remembered what we had before that night, who he used to be.

"And now? We're back. My records are here. We aren't erased anymore."

"Yeah. My guess is the same people who scrubbed our existence in this town changed their mind." Her voice dropped to a whisper. "We're here because they demanded we come back... so long as we play by the rules."

I laughed, bitter and broken. "We don't do rules."

"We do now."

A long pause.

"Why didn't you tell me before?" I asked, my voice raw.

"Because knowing makes you a liability. And I couldn't risk that. Not when they already have everything."

"They don't have me."

She didn't respond. Didn't have to. Because we both knew they had me too. They had the school. Her job. Our future on a leash. I swallowed, forcing my voice to steady. "Is this about Luke? Is that why you panicked when you realized I'm not upset about Elise. That... it's about him?"

Her voice cracked then. Barely a whisper: "Stay away from him, Mila. That family's not safe."

"I already knew that." But I refused to believe Luke was the same.

"No. You don't."

Blackwood had always been a gilded cage. Now I knew just how deep the trap went. I fell to the bed and rested my back against the headboard and closed my eyes. I was caught between two wars. One from the past—and one barreling straight for me.

"He's not the same as them," I whispered. More to myself than her.

She reached for my hand. "You sure?"

I didn't answer.

She stayed a while longer, her hand wrapped around mine. When she finally left, I stared at the ceiling, the truth pressing down, a storm heavy in my chest.

Luke didn't know. He couldn't. But he would. Because despite everything, even the lie I'd told myself earlier, I wasn't done giving him a chance—not yet.

CHAPTER THIRTY-TWO

LUKE

I'd driven aimlessly last night after talking with my brother—just thinking. Trying to figure out my next move. And I had. I was still angry about the way she'd left a year ago. Maybe she couldn't tell me everything—but that had to end. Her reaching out, sharing with me what she had, meant something. A step toward rebuilding what she'd torched when she walked away. And maybe a bridge for us to stand on now. Maybe even build something new. Goddammit, I wanted that. We just had to figure out how.

The morning at school hadn't gone the way I'd planned. Every time I got close, she bolted. Or had Avery flanking her, a shield at her side.

Then I spotted her outside the locker rooms right before gym. She leaned against the wall, scrolling on her phone, her posture loose but guarded.

The hallway was chaos. People moved in waves. Laughter, slamming lockers, background noise. But she was still. And alone. No Avery. No exit route. Just her. And a chance.

The guys had been reading my mood all morning. So when they spotted Mila, not much needed to be said.

"I'll catch up," was all I gave them.

They nodded, didn't press, and kept walking. I turned back to her. When I was in front of her, I stepped in close and braced my hand against the wall just above her head, creating a small pocket of space—closed off from the noise, the stares. "Mila." Her name caught in the air between us.

Her eyes flicked to me. Wary. Guarded. Wounded. All of it captured in that tilt of her head, framed by amber lights overhead.

"I was wrong." The words were low, meant only for her. "You brought me information tied to my family—and I pushed you away. I shouldn't have."

She held my gaze. Didn't blink.

I swallowed. "I hurt you when you were trying to help. Thought I was being careful—rational. But I didn't see what it cost you." My hand flexed against the wall, the fingers at my side curling into a fist to stop from touching her. "And I made it worse. Not better."

She shifted. Took a breath. "Why the change in perspective now?"

"Because you took a risk." I kept my voice steady despite the weight behind it. "I can't undo how I handled it. Only how things happen going forward."

She studied me then raised her hand slowly, resting it flat against my chest—right over my heart. Her fingers didn't tremble. They pressed in, steady. Not soft. "Words don't fix what's broken."

"I know." My voice was rough. "So here's mine." I leaned in, just enough to close the distance. My breath skimmed her skin —close, not touching.

I wasn't blocking her in completely—my body angled, shoulder turned toward the hall. From there, I caught movement as Elise passed. Her gaze flicked to where Mila's hand was pressed to my chest. She didn't say anything—just absorbed the moment, storing it as a weapon for later.

"I'm sorry. For not trusting you. For the rejection when you tried to give me information that mattered. For hurting you. I'm not asking for a chance. I'll just show you what I would do with one."

Silence swelled. Lockers slammed, feet shuffled, voices drifted. But in our space—just breath and the weight of everything unsaid.

She didn't move. Then slowly, she lifted her head, her eyes meeting mine, steady and unreadable.

"Saying you were wrong means something," she said quietly. "But it doesn't undo what it did."

"I know." My chest tightened. "We should talk. Really talk."

She studied me then gave a small nod. No promise. Just a maybe.

I took it and ran. "Meet me on the arena roof. Tonight. After practice."

She didn't answer. Just stepped out from under my arm and walked toward the locker rooms. I stayed there long after the bell. Because all I saw was Mila.

CHAPTER THIRTY-THREE

MILA

I spent the rest of gym class trying not to think about Luke's promise. Every whistle, every echoing thump of a basket-ball, every squeak of shoes against the floor was a drumbeat telling me something had shifted. It wasn't just the apology—it was that he meant it. And maybe that meant we weren't done.

Teachers droned on in my classes, one after another, but not a word registered. History, English, science—they all swirled in the background while my mind replayed everything Luke said.

Avery had tried—quietly during lunch. She caught my hand beneath the table, asking what had happened. I wasn't ready to share. I gave her a half-smile and watched the hallway, telling myself later I'd talk. But I didn't. Not yet.

It wasn't until the end of my favorite class—Advanced Studio—after the bell rang that I felt it. Relief. The only room I wanted to be in anymore was the studio. Not school. Not home. Somewhere I could untangle space and color, somewhere I could start again.

A few steps later, Avery plopped beside me at one of the metal-topped tables, her sketchbook splayed open in front of her. "Honestly," she muttered, "I can't draw worth a damn."

She tapped at a half-finished figure wrestling with perspective. "I tried sketching—guess who?" She'd been doodling what suspiciously resembled Jax: square jaw, stormy eyes, hunched hockey posture. A decent likeness, all things considered.

I glanced over. "That's... actually not bad."

She grimaced. "It's awful. Look—I messed up the ear, the jaw's wonky, and the damn eyes are off-kilter."

I leaned in. "Here, try softening the jawline—less square, more angular. And shift the eye over a bit." I traced the adjustment on the page. "There. Now he looks like trouble, the kind you want to chase."

She blinked, a smile creeping in. "That's... kinda better." She pushed her hair back. "See? I'm totally the worst artist in the room."

I rolled my eyes. "You're not, Aves."

She laughed quietly, nudging me. "Shut up and let me finish it."

We sat there—two artists lost in the rhythm of lines, hearts tangled in places pencils couldn't reach.

I stayed late after the bell rang to finish a sketch—of Luke, of course—before packing up. The hallway lights were warm, yellowed glass, the corridor empty of students. I thumbed through Luke's text: *Roof. After practice.*

I dumped the books I wouldn't need into my locker, spun the dial, and turned to leave—then stopped cold.

Elise's voice. Muffled. Clipped. Laced with venom.

I took a step toward the bathroom entrance then paused just before the corner. I tried to convince myself that I wasn't hiding. I wasn't eavesdropping. But I didn't move. Didn't breathe. Because something in her tone said I needed to hear this.

"I'm trying! He's chasing her—what do you want me to do, drug him?"

My breath caught in my chest. She wasn't laughing. She

sounded angry, scared, and unhinged. I backed away, putting some distance between myself and the door, nearer the girls' basketball trophy case where she might not see me.

Elise flew through the girls' bathroom door, storming toward the school's exit without seeing me. I waited then crept forward and checked around the corner. No one. She'd been on the phone.

A second later, she slapped both palms into the metal bar on the exit door, shoving it open before disappearing from sight. Then came the silence. A hollow, echoing quiet that somehow roared louder than her voice.

My stomach rolled as the world spun around me—What if she meant it? What if she wasn't kidding?

The crack in her composure felt darker than high school petty. This wasn't drama. This was desperation. A girl coming undone under pressure. And whatever she'd been asked to do... it had pushed her too far.

I backed out of the corridor, legs heavy, mind reeling. The halls had mostly emptied, the last stragglers filtering toward the parking lot. At the exit, I paused long enough to check my phone.

One message blinked from Avery: *You good? You seemed off all day.*

I typed back: *Yeah. Just needed a minute.*

No explanation. She'd probably already left, assuming I would catch up later.

I took the long way out. Climbed into my car and drove without thinking—muscle memory steering me toward the only place that ever made sense when the noise got too loud—the studio at the boardwalk.

I parked, climbed over the sand-stained railing, and walked until the spray kissed my ankles. Waves slapped the pilings. A breeze tangled through my hair.

Then I called Mom. Fingertips shaking. She answered on the

third ring, and mind spinning, I jumped right into my latest problem. "You're not going to—Elise didn't—I mean..." I paused, swallowed.

"Slow down, Mila. What happened?"

When I told her what I'd overheard, her voice went low.

"Look." Mom's tone was measured but urgent. "All I can speculate is that her father's putting the screws to her. I've only heard rumors, but the man's ruthless. Elise might be under pressure to find a weakness in the Kings, and fast. Whether it's her dad pushing that angle or someone else—I don't know. But it tracks."

The spray cooled my skin, but the burn inside stayed hot. "She said 'drug him.' Like she meant it."

"I'm hoping that was desperation talking. Not a plan." Her voice stayed even, but I could hear the tight thread underneath. "These people don't care about consequences. They deal in perception and power. My guess is if she thinks a rumor, or a threat, will do damage—she might run with it. Just to get leverage. I hope not drugs."

I stared at the water, my pulse skipping. "That's not leverage. That's psychotic."

"Mila, when girls like Elise fall apart, they don't just cry— they cut everyone around them."

I couldn't tell if Elise had meant it—if it was a threat or just fury bleeding through pressure. But I knew one thing for sure— the girl I'd just overheard wasn't scheming; she was spiraling. Desperate. Someone cracking under the weight of expectations she couldn't carry anymore.

I exhaled. "Mom, I need to tell Luke what I heard. And about Dunn." I flinched, realizing I'd already done that last night. "And about me, why we left in the first place."

Silence. Then, "Honey, be smart. He's a King. We don't really know what side he's on, but I doubt it's ours."

I exhaled hard, deciding she might not need to carry the

weight of all my confessions. "Mom, I'm going to tell him what I overheard. And about Elise." What I left out was I was going to tell him everything.

Her silence stretched. "That's your call. Just... be smart." Her voice was soft. Protective. It wasn't permission. But it wasn't discouragement either.

I turned away from the water and walked back to my car. I'd driven here to think. Now it was time to decide.

I wasn't sure how Luke would take it. That we came back for reasons we'd hidden. That we were entangled in something bigger. But he'd risked something real for me today—he deserved the truth.

The waves hissed behind me, and I drew in a breath. *I'm going to tell him.*

It was the beginning of honesty. Because if we were going to build anything from the wreckage... we needed to know exactly what we were building.

CHAPTER THIRTY-FOUR

LUKE

Practice was over. The locker room was quiet. For once. No shouting. No gear clattering. No barking from Coach. Just the distant hum of the lights and the low thud of blood in my ears.

I sat on the bench, elbows on my knees, gear bag at my feet. My fingers hesitated over the small zippered flap on the inside pocket. The one I hadn't opened in months. Maybe longer.

I didn't know why I reached for it now. Maybe I'd run out of other distractions. Or maybe I already knew what I would find.

I slid the zipper down and reached in. Felt the cool press of metal against my fingers. When I pulled it out, it was just as I remembered. A white-gold chain. Thin. Barely there. And dangling from the center—a single star. I didn't breathe for a second. Just stared at it. Let the weight of it settle in my palm.

She never told me she'd left it. Didn't need to. I'd found it right before a game—months after she disappeared. Just a glint of metal buried beneath mouth guards and tape. I didn't ask how it got there. I didn't tell anyone I kept it. I just… did. It felt like the only piece of her that hadn't vanished when she did— even if leaving it behind was its own message.

I pressed the charm between my fingers now, thumb brushing over the edges as if summoning her from memory.

This necklace was everything—a reminder of that night on the roof. Of the shooting star that cut across the sky, a promise we didn't know how to keep. Of a dream whispered into darkness. It was a symbol of distance. Of fate. Of something bigger than us—but still undeniably *us*.

I stared at it and asked myself the question I hadn't dared before. Could we survive this time? Could we hold on long enough to rewrite what we broke? Or would the chaos swallowing us—family, secrets, expectations—tear us apart all over again?

I didn't have the answer. But I clenched the necklace in my fist, held it tight as if it still meant something. Because it did. Because she did. Even if I couldn't say it out loud yet.

For so long, I'd told myself I was over her. That Mila Callahan was just a scar I'd learned to live with. But the proof sat in my hand. Thin chain. Small star. Every lie I'd fed myself burned away in the weight of it.

If I opened my fist and she left again, I wouldn't crawl back out this time. There'd be nothing left to put back together.

The air in the locker room pressed heavy, metallic, suffocating. I bent forward, necklace biting my palm, breath dragging rough through my chest. I hated how easy it would be to follow her if she ran again.

That was the real weakness. Not her leaving. Me.

I tucked the necklace in my pocket, shouldered my bag, and headed up to the roof, thumbing off a text to Mila: *I'm up. Meet me.*

It was getting late, and my stomach growled, but I didn't move. I wasn't leaving this roof until I saw her. Until I knew.

The chain in my pocket was featherlight. But it carried weight—what it meant. What it could still—a new beginning. Or maybe just the illusion of one.

The sky hadn't tipped into full dark yet—just a dim gray blur overhead. Not enough stars. But the remnants of our past were already here. It clung to this rooftop, waiting for us to finish the story we left half-burned.

There were memories up here. They breathed. They lingered in the cracks of the concrete and in the way the air smelled of rain and ash. I wanted more of them. The question was whether we could ever outrun the distrust that simmered between us.

The door squeaked open behind me, that familiar shriek of metal on metal. I turned just as Mila slipped through the doorway. Same jeans. Same dark waves whipping behind her. She moved—both warning and a promise—closing the space until she stood a foot away. Close enough that I could smell her shampoo. Not close enough to invite touch. That single foot between us had never felt so far away.

"I wasn't sure you would show." My voice was rougher than I wanted.

She shrugged. Looked away. Then locked determined gray-green eyes with mine. "You made amends for your colossal fuckup." Her full lips twitched, bitter amusement curling them for a split second before she masked it again.

"Before I tell you why I really came," she said, voice edged with hesitation, "there's something you need to know. I overheard Elise on the phone. I couldn't catch the whole conversation, but she made it sound as though her job is to get you back, her role in whatever's going on. There was a dangerous desperation to her voice. Drugging you was flung out as a last resort."

That was a new one. But impossible. I wouldn't accept anything from her, or her friends. Still, the thought of Elise desperate enough to consider it scraped like glass under my ribs. I forced my tone flat. "Elise is a nonstarter. She doesn't matter. Never did."

She didn't flinch. "Maybe not to you. But don't write her off.

She's a pawn in this game—and not a random one. She's tied to the companies. You know which ones I mean."

I did. And the knot in my gut tightened. Pawns weren't harmless. Pawns were how the board shifted without anyone noticing. "I appreciate the warning. But Elise can't get close to me. I'm not worried about her."

"Okay." Her lips pressed together. "Then we can move on. Because the rest of what I have to say… it's bigger. And I need to know you're not going to stab me in the back."

That one resonated. Probably because I'd earned it. But she wasn't blameless either. "That's a tall order coming from you, based on your prior actions."

She grimaced. "Right. I get that. Thing is, I didn't have all the details before. I do now." She lifted her hand, palm out, warding me off. "And I know it's asking a lot—but I do need your promise. That whatever I say, you'll protect me and my mom. You won't do anything that'll put us in the crosshairs."

I stilled. She was asking for everything. But after last night? After the olive branch she'd offered? "You have my word."

Her breath left in a gust. Her shoulders slumped just enough to prove she hadn't been sure I'd say it.

I reached for her hand and pulled her toward the blanket I'd laid out. Old habit. Familiar pattern. Her raised brow told me she recognized it too. We sat. Close but not quite touching. And then she leaned forward and unraveled everything.

"I was never able to tell you why we'd left." Her fingers twisted a strand of her long hair, lips pressed tight. "I don't even remember why I had to meet Mom at work that night. Doesn't matter. I followed her location. When I got there…" Her body shuddered. "There was blood. A body. We got the hell out. Back at our place, she wouldn't tell me who pulled the trigger. Just… hinted. Enough to buy my silence."

My stomach coiled.

"This town has a ruling order," she whispered. "And crossing them? That would've been fatal."

My lungs stalled. My family *was* the ruling order. "What are you saying, Mila?"

"I just need you to listen, okay?"

Cold seeped into my bones, but I gave her a single nod. It cost more than I let on.

"The person who was killed... it was my mom's boyfriend. Darren Langley."

My throat closed. "The VP?"

She nodded. "We fled that night. No packing. No warning. Mom didn't even let me reach out. She wasn't sure if we'd been seen."

None of it made sense. "If she was afraid of my family, why come back?" Mila never outright said one of us pulled the trigger, and I wasn't sure I wanted to ask, or that I was willing to believe it could be true. There had to be another explanation, and maybe she didn't have the whole story.

"What was going on before we left, that I just recently found out about, was that our names were being scrubbed. From school. Medical. Emergency contacts. Like we'd never existed."

I exhaled sharply.

She pressed on. "Darren got curious. Started digging where he shouldn't. Told Mom what he'd found. Two days later, he was dead." A tremor rolled through her. "That's why we ran. Before whoever it was decided we were next."

Her throat worked, her eyes darting away before snapping back to mine. "There's something else. My mom... she saw Lorne that night. Standing over Darren's body. Gun in hand. She swears he didn't see her. And by the time I got there, he was already gone. But it was enough. Too much. She panicked. We both did. Telling the cops wasn't an option, not if they were already in your family's pocket. The risk was too great to stay."

It was a gut punch. Heat drained, my chest iced over, leaving something jagged.

Lorne. Not blood. But close enough. My dad's shadow at every dinner. His name stamped on contracts. His hand steady on my shoulder after wins, after losses. A constant.

And in Mila's memory—standing over a body with a gun.

The denial clawed at me, sharp and useless. But it didn't hold. Because deep down, I believed her.

If it was true, then every handshake, every deal, every scrap of trust I'd given him was rotten. He wasn't outside the walls. He was already inside them.

Which meant Mila wasn't in danger of some faceless enemy. She was in danger of the man my family kept inviting closer. The man I'd let too close.

My pulse crashed. Because if she was right, then I couldn't protect her. Not from him. Not from the people sitting at my own table. Not even from myself.

The image of him waiting for me after practice slammed into place—how he'd intercepted me, all calm authority, and handed me the paperwork for the boardwalk studio with his signature on the sale's approval. I thought it'd been a test. Now, I knew better. He'd been giving me a message. That Mila was already in his sights. And everything snapped into place with a sickening click.

"There must be some mistake." Hollow words. "You're here now. Your records are back. No one's coming after you."

"There's a reason for that." She released the hair she twisted and then threaded her hands together until her knuckles turned white. "They made Mom come back. Blackmailed her into returning. But only if we play by the rules." She leaned forward even more and settled a hand against my chest. Her fingers splayed wide over my heart.

"That's why I can't hit back at Elise. Not the way I want to." Her voice cracked. "My mom works for her father now. If I push too far, it blows back on both of us." She swallowed hard. "We're stuck playing by rules we don't even understand. And I don't want to have to leave again. My mom promised we would stay this time. Long enough for me to graduate from Blackwood Academy. It's better than running again. Better for my future. So I keep my head down. Bite my tongue. Most of the time. Even when it kills me."

"Who is *they*?"

She shrugged. "I-I don't know for sure. Only that Mom told me to stay away from you. Said your family's not safe."

I stared at her. At everything she wasn't saying. At everything she was afraid to. Then I dropped the match. "Darren isn't dead."

Her breath caught.

"There was never any notice about his death. No news, no whispers. Your mom doesn't have the full story."

Her jaw twitched, eyes shuttered. "You said you would trust me. Give me the benefit of the doubt."

"I did. I do. Look… if there was a cover-up, and he *is* dead? Then I get why your mom ran." I leaned back slightly, just enough to get a clearer look at her, and her hand fell away. I missed the warmth of it instantly. "But, Mila… I was told your mom stole from us."

Guilt flickered in her eyes before quickly vanishing. "I—I don't know about that. Maybe she stole from her boyfriend. I don't think it was from your family's company."

"Okay." Something was off there, but that part wasn't what I needed to focus on. It didn't matter right now. What did was that someone had painted a target on her back. "You need to keep your head down." My instincts were screaming at me to do something, protect her, keep her safe. "Don't poke the beast. Don't give them a reason."

Her lips parted as if she had more to say. But she didn't. Not yet. Not about that.

"And what about us?" she whispered.

Fuck. I had her in my sights. Always had. It didn't matter if we were fighting, ignoring each other, or on opposite sides of the battlefield. She walked into a room, and my body went up in flames. "I've got your back," I said. "We'll figure this out. But we do it together."

She waited a beat then nodded, her gaze locked on mine. "Together."

"No more secrets."

"That goes both ways." Her voice dropped to a dare.

"We're in agreement then. A team."

She nodded. And I was done pretending.

I surged forward, one hand slipping behind her neck, fingers tangling in her silky hair. Her breath caught, and then I kissed her. Hard. My mouth crashed into hers like we'd been on a collision course from the start. She opened for me instantly, lips parting, as though she'd been holding this in as long as I had.

Her taste hit me—salt and heat and something wild I couldn't name. My other hand slid to her waist, tightening as I lifted her. She moved without hesitation, straddling my lap like she belonged there. Her hands clutched my shirt, twisting, anchoring. Her body pressed to mine, hips rocking with urgency I felt in every bone.

Every sound she made lit me up like gasoline to a fuse. I kissed her as if I was starving—because I was. For her. For this. For the fucking truth between us finally getting air.

Her fingers found the back of my neck, tugging me closer, as if even this wasn't enough. And maybe it wasn't. Not with everything we'd buried. Everything we'd denied.

When we finally came up for air, our foreheads touched. Her lips were swollen, breath hitching. Her eyes dazed but clear. A crooked grin tugged at her mouth.

"This changes things."

"Damn right it does." I went in again. Slower. Deeper. More

of a claim than a kiss. She moaned into my mouth and arched against me.

A car horn blared below. We froze. Then pulled apart, reluctantly.

The sky had turned indigo above us, stars scattered, confessions written in light. I reached into my pocket. Pulled out the chain. "Might as well mark the night."

She blinked, her eyes going suspiciously shiny. "You kept it?"

I didn't answer. Just brushed her hair aside and clasped the chain around her neck. Her fingers drifted up, grazing the tiny silver star. It settled just above her collarbone.

"I left it in your bag the night of the game," she whispered. "For luck. I wasn't supposed to leave that night. I thought I'd be there to get it back from you the next day."

Her revelation hit me, a shock wave down my spine. She hadn't meant to disappear. The necklace wasn't a goodbye—it was a thread we never got to finish. It changed things.

"Still suits you," I murmured. I wanted to claim her. Make her mine. Shout it to the world. But we couldn't do that, not yet. Not with my family's warning in my ears and Lorne standing like a shadow at the edge of everything.

She touched the star, voice low and steady. "We can't be reckless. Not with this. Not with us. If they find out…"

"I know." The words scraped out of me. "We keep it quiet. Off their radar. Allies. Partners."

Her eyes didn't waver. "Not lovers. Not yet. But don't think for a second I'm shutting this down. Not again."

I swallowed hard. The heat between us wasn't going anywhere. "Then we fight smart. Together. And whatever this is"—I brushed the star at her collarbone—"we keep it ours until it's safe to burn the rest of the world with it."

Not just friends. Not enemies. And not what we were before. Something volatile. A secret. A truce painted in starlight and skin.

She didn't answer. Didn't need to. Because that star? That kiss? That promise? They weren't just ours now. They were war paint. And we would need it.

Want to know out what happens with Luke and Mila? To find out, continue reading the Blackwood Blades series with CROSS-CHECK.

Thanks so much for reading my work. If you enjoyed reading ICED OUT, I hope you'll consider leaving a review or rating.

If you liked Iced Out, check out the Hidden Valley Elite series.

Looking for your next book to read? Check out more books by Amy McKinley/Isla Vaughn here: https://store.amymckinleyauthor.com/pages/reading-order

ACKNOWLEDGMENTS

This story refused to stay quiet—it demanded to be written, twisting, colliding, and consuming until I finally gave in. I could never have carried it to the finish line without some extraordinary people who kept me standing when the words got heavy.

To my family—you've learned to recognize the look in my eyes when I disappear into a fictional storm, and still you give me space to chase it. Thank you for never questioning the early hour writing sessions, the frantic deadlines, and the endless cups of coffee. Your love and support are my anchor.

To my critique partners—you already know how much you mean to me. You listen when I ramble, talk me down when I panic, and push me when I need it most. This time, you went above and beyond—jumping in on an impossibly tight deadline, giving your time and energy when I needed it most. Candace Irving, Emily Albright, Kristin Kisska, and Jessica Riley Miller— thank you for showing up in the trenches again and again. Your honesty, brilliance, and generosity make every book stronger, but more than that, your friendship makes this wild ride possible.

To my editor, Taylor Anhalt—your sharp eye and tireless patience are a gift. You catch what I miss, challenge me to dig deeper, and somehow help me polish chaos into clarity. This book is better because of you, and I'm endlessly thankful for the care and heart you pour into every page.

To my illustrator, Audrey Anhalt—thank you for giving

Luke and Mila a face, a presence, a heartbeat before a single word is read. That cover captures their tension and tenderness so beautifully. And to TE Black Designs—you worked your magic yet again, transforming vision into a final cover design that took my breath away.

Colleen Noyes and the team at Itsy Bitsy Book Bits—you never stop championing authors with passion and dedication. I'm grateful for every ounce of energy you pour into connecting readers with the stories they'll love.

And finally—to the readers. Whether you've been with me from the beginning or just picked this one up, thank you for taking a chance on my words. Your enthusiasm, your reviews, your emails—they are the reason I can keep doing this. If you haven't yet, come join my newsletter crew—because this ride is just getting started.

With so much love and gratitude—thank you.

ABOUT THE AUTHOR

Isla Vaughn writes steamy sports romance packed with fierce women, irresistible alpha males, and all the emotional chaos in between. She's the author of the *Hidden Valley Elite* series and several other sports romance series. When she's not writing, she's probably reading, drinking too much coffee, or dreaming about life in a beach house.

instagram.com/islavaughnauthor
facebook.com/author.IslaVaughn
tiktok.com/@islavaughnauthor
bookbub.com/profile/isla-vaughn
goodreads.com/islavaughn_author

ALSO BY ISLA VAUGHN

Hidden Valley Elite Series

Savage Start

Savage Lies

Savage Truth

Brutal Days

Brutal Nights

Cruel Start

Cruel Hate

Cruel Love

Wicked Games

Wicked Ends

Fall Lake Ballers

Quarterback Keeper

Pump Fake

Red Zone

Power Plays & Pucks

Shattered Ice

Pucking Power Plays *(coming soon)*

Blackwood Blades *(coming soon)*

Iced Out

Cross-Check

Sudden Death

Isla Vaughn also publishes under *USA Today* bestselling author Amy McKinley.

Mafia Elite

No Way Out

Blood Oath

Born in Darkness

Savage Secrets

Ruthless Heir

Collateral Damage

Rivals

Gray Ghost Novels (Former Navy SEALs)

Moments That Define Us

Broken Circle

Eye of the Storm

Beneath the Surface

Vantage Point

Covert Threat

Marked for Death

Deadly Isles Special Ops (Navy SEALs)

Twisted Secrets

Bound by Secrets

Forged by Secrets

Standalone Titles

Shattered Melody

Siren's Call: Cursed Seas

Fake Fiancé (A Second Chance Office Romance)

Moonlit Destination Series

Moonlit Whisper

Moonlit Kiss

Moonlit Mirage

Five Fates Series

Hidden

Taken

Bound by Blood Mafia Series *(coming soon)*

Hidde Enemy

Stolen Prize

Secret Pawn

Broken Vow

Buried Rival

Tarnished Crown